D1377776

GOOD STORIES REVEAL as much, or more, about a locale as any map or guidebook. Whereabouts Press is dedicated to publishing books that will enlighten a traveler to the soul of a place. By bringing a country's stories to the English-speaking reader, we hope to convey its culture through literature. Books from Whereabouts Press are essential companions for the curious traveler, and for the person who appreciates how fine writing enhances one's experiences in the world.

"Coming newly into Spanish, I lacked two essentials—a childhood in the language, which I could never acquire, and a sense of its literature, which I could."

—Alastair Reid, *Whereabouts:
Notes on Being a Foreigner*

OTHER TRAVELER'S LITERARY COMPANIONS

FORTHCOMING:

FRANCE

A TRAVELER'S LITERARY COMPANION

EDITED BY

WILLIAM RODARMOR
AND ANNA LIVIA

WHEREABOUTS PRESS
BERKELEY, CALIFORNIA

Copyright © 2008 by Whereabouts Press

Preface © 2008 by William Rodarmor
(complete copyright information on page 243)

Map of France by Bill Nelson

Published by
Whereabouts Press
Berkeley, California
www.whereaboutspress.com

Distributed to the trade by PGW / Perseus Distribution

MANUFACTURED IN THE UNITED STATES OF AMERICA

Library of Congress Cataloging-in-Publication Data
France : a traveler's literary companion /
edited by William Rodarmor and Anna Livia.
p.   cm. — (Travelers literary companions ; 16)
ISBN-13: 978-1-883513-18-4 (alk. paper)
ISBN-10: 1-883513-18-9 (alk. paper)
1. Short stories, French—Translations into English.
2. French fiction—21st century—Translations into English.
3. France—Fiction. I. Rodarmor, William. II. Livia, Anna.
PQ1278.F68   2008
843'.0108—dc22
2008022099

5 4 3 2 1

Contents

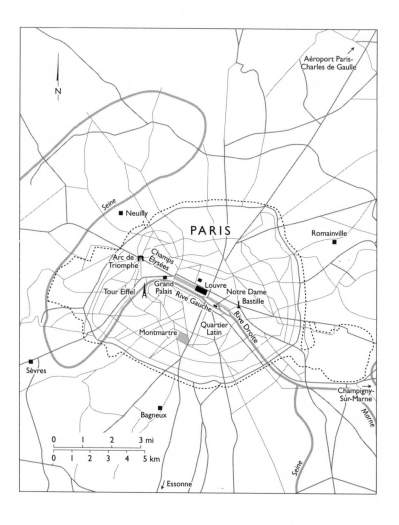

Preface

Oddly enough, the French word *cliché* doesn't mean "cliché," the way we use it in English. It means snapshot, which is a good place to start when thinking about a country imagined almost entirely in clichés. Quick: What comes to mind when you hear the word "France"? Paris and the Eiffel Tower? Good food, snooty waiters, and dogs in restaurants? The Resistance, chain-smoking kids, Cartier-Bresson photographs? Astérix, Charles de Gaulle, the Normandy beaches? Though clichés, these all contain an underlying grain of truth. And it's interesting how different they are from each other. Not surprising if you consider that France has as wide a range of landscapes and people as the United States, all squeezed into a country the size of Texas.

France has another distinction, though it is not unique. Like England and Russia, it's intensely capital-conscious. A map of French highways and railroad lines looks like a diagram of the nerves and blood vessels, with the brain and heart right in the center, on the banks of the Seine. Take a French train from anywhere A to anyplace B, and there's a fair chance it will enter Paris at the Gare du Nord and leave from Gare Montparnasse. Parisians speak of "the provinces," but so do the provincials in Bordeaux and Lyon.

When you set out to explore France, whether on foot or in your imagination, it's always fun to start in Paris. It's not called the City of Light for nothing, and its charms are considerable. But if Paris is where good Americans go when they die, as Oscar Wilde said, that leaves the rest of France to those of us who are less good and more venturesome.

So, free yourself from Paris's seductive embrace, and move beyond its *boulevards périphériques,* which sounds so much nicer than "bypass" or "ring road." (Professor Higgins in *My Fair Lady:* "The French don't care what you do, actually, so long as you pronounce it properly.") Travel a few miles out of the city, and you discover why the word "suburb" doesn't quite work in France. Sure, Paris has leafy middle-class exurbs, like the one where Christian Lehmann says he became a bookish young criminal. But it also has gritty slums and backwaters of urban anomie— just ask Samuel Benchetrit or Frédéric Fajardie.

Next, go south for a swirl of sunshine and mystery with stories by Colette, Pierre Magnan, Le Clézio, and especially François Maspero, who lends mythic dimensions to a 1942 train trip along the coast of Provence. Head west, and catch the chill wind off the Atlantic Ocean and the English Channel. Annie Ernaux and Eric Holder describe women whose attitudes or appearances make them profoundly alien to their birthplaces. Jean Failler and Anna Gavalda enjoy laughing at their characters' expense, albeit in the nicest possible way.

East of Paris lie history and remembrance, war-ravaged

fields with new grass and old memories. The stories by Gabriel Chevallier and Marcel Aymé are humorous tales of country life, but those by Annie Saumont and Didier Daeninckx are war stories, and they toll a deeper tone. Finally, Dominique Jamet takes us on his personal Tour de France, a voyage of the mind in which his hero is always homeward bound.

For an editor, choosing a handful of stories to represent a country as complex as France is no easy task. That said, many of the stories in this volume do fall into recognizable patterns. My late coeditor, Anna Livia, picked Marcel Aymé's country classic "The Dogs in Our Life," so I paired it with Luc Lang's "Dog Mind," which is about the sticky problem of dogs in the city. Because of the jarring contrast in their suburban settings, I also chose two stories about stealing, "The Book Thief" and "An Ear for an Ear." In general I looked for stories with roots, ones like the truffles in Pierre Magnan's "Garcinets Pass," which will grow nowhere else.

Short-story writers are often urged by their publishers to write "real" books, that is, novels. French authors may be under special pressure, with towering novelists like Balzac and Zola casting long shadows across their bookshelves. Also, it's been argued that France doesn't have as venerable a short-story tradition as England or Russia. A *nouvelle*, as it's called, is viewed as a sketch or an anecdote, and the very word suggests a piece of news more than a work of literature.

In fact, writers from Jules Verne to Albert Camus by way of Alphonse Daudet and Prosper Mérimée have written wonderful short stories. Guy de Maupassant was probably the master of the form, and gave the world the deathless phrase "Mademoiselle Fifi." Ironically, de Maupassant was so prolific that some of his contemporaries considered him a hack. But examine one of those stories, and you'll see that it's constructed as ingeniously as clockwork.

Short-story authors revel in a form that gives the writer the greatest freedom and the most constraint, and many prefer it to novels. As Annie Saumont, the grande dame of the modern French short story, said in a recent interview, "Whenever I set out to write a novel, it always ends in about ten pages."

When one of these masters gets to work, it's like watching a magician pull rabbits out of a hat, except that instead of rabbits, they're mynah birds, or maybe parrots, each speaking in a distinctive voice. Like France itself, their variety is amazing.

I hope this collection does justice to that variety. Some of the stories are funny, some are sad, a few are mysterious. The excerpts may seem to end too soon, but that's all to the good. These pieces are neither bonbons nor full-course meals. They're more like hearty appetizers. You're at a bountiful buffet, and you should feel free to come back for more.

William Rodarmor
Berkeley, California

The Book Thief

Christian Lehmann

I STARTED STEALING BOOKS very early.

Which is why I now had a major case of the shits. I was twelve years old, and I was sitting slumped over on the toilet seat, my forehead damp with sweat, my ears ringing; I could hear my father raging through the closed door. I could hear snatches of phrases borne along with the street noises and the commuter train screeching to a stop at the Bellevue Station: ". . . little bastard . . . makes no sense . . . after all we've done for him . . . really look like an idiot . . ."

I felt no shame, no remorse, but I was mortified. For months, I'd been waiting for the inevitable moment when my father would discover what I'd been up to. But I had

CHRISTIAN LEHMANN (1958–) is a medical doctor, writer, and political activist on health issues. Among other books, he is the author of the bestseller *No pasarán, le jeu* (1996, tr. *Ultimate Game*), its sequel, *Andreas, le retour* (2005), and *Patients, si vous saviez* (2003). His latest book is *Sarkolangue* (2008), a biting analysis of President Nicolas Sarkozy's policies. This is an excerpt from Lehmann's 2000 autobiography, *Une education anglaise*.

imagined that I would feel the storm coming and have time to allay his suspicions. It hadn't turned out that way. My brother's treachery had done me in.

I flushed the toilet and went out into the hallway. A quick glance to the left, into the bedroom I shared with my brother, Daniel, told me the extent of the damage. My father had dumped the entire contents of the wooden bookshelves onto my bed. Books, comic books, and magazines were heaped on the bright orange bedspread, and I couldn't repress a feeling of pleased surprise when I realized that, except for one or two *Spirou* comics my father had dutifully paid for, I had stolen all the rest.

The bedroom was empty, so I ran toward the kitchen to take refuge behind my mother's skirts. The apartment was a narrow one, and my father was standing in the living room, waiting for me to finish emptying my bowels. When he saw me, he shouted, "Christian!"

I burst into the kitchen, my heart pounding. My mother turned to me, smiling absently. She was fixing Sunday lunch and listening to the radio, whose programs wavered between decades-long kowtowing to the establishment and the new boldness of the 1970s. My mother knew full well that the media had been in the hands of the Reds since the events of May 1968, but she took a perverse pleasure in listening anyway, the better to fulminate against the Trotskyite-Leninist conspiracy threatening the free world.

"Christian!" screamed my father again.

I had a fierce urge to vomit, to piss, to melt into some nauseating pool of liquid.

"Your father's calling you, darling. Didn't you hear him?"

My mother continued what she was doing, as if unaware of the psychodrama unfolding in my bedroom a dozen yards away. Her playful, casual tone affected me even more deeply than my father's anger. It was as if she'd been left standing on the platform while the runaway train of my downfall roared toward a final cataclysm. She was part of my previous life, the one in which I was a precocious high-school freshman at the Sèvres international lycée. She didn't yet know about her son's new personality—the juvenile delinquent, the suburban sneak, the book thief.

"Christian!"

My father burst into the kitchen, looking pale and ugly. My mother stopped what she was doing and asked, "What's the matter?"

Her face had suddenly crumpled, and I felt overwhelmed by a wave of shame. Not shame at what I'd done, but shame at being the cause of her transformation.

"What's the matter? The matter is that your son is a thief!"

My mother put her hands to her lips, just like in the movies. I couldn't speak, couldn't defend myself, couldn't look at her. My father dragged me into my bedroom. Seen up close, the heap of my stolen goods looked even more impressive. Daniel was sitting at his desk and pretending to do his geography homework, without missing a scrap of the unfolding drama.

"There's hundreds of francs' worth of stuff here! Maybe

thousands," yelled my father. "How could you do something like this? How could you?"

Actually, it had been pretty easy. Like taking candy from a baby.

Thinking back on it now, I'm amazed that it went for so long without my being caught. By the time my father discovered the extent of my crimes, nearly nine months had passed since I stole my first book. Nine months during which I had "shopped" at the town bookstore every day except Saturdays, Sundays, and holidays, practically without spending a centime. The script never varied. I would take the bus in front of the lycée, get off downtown, and walk by the bookstore twice to see how many customers were inside. It was all a matter of instinct. I needed enough people to keep the bookseller and her assistants busy, but not too many because my little sleight of hand required a little privacy. The ideal was seven or eight customers. If there were more than a dozen, it wasn't worth attempting.

As a book thief, I had a great deal going for me. Besides colossal nerve, I looked like a cross between the smartest boy in the class and a worshipful shepherd gazing at the baby Jesus. I was small and frail, always dragging a school bag that (for good reason) was too heavy for me. I probably moved the bookstore staff to tears on the rare occasions when I approached the cash register clutching some one-franc coins in one hand and my latest find in the other. I was an outstanding reader and a perfect customer— aside from my stealing, of course. As the years went by, they had seen me rummaging through their shelves for hours. By the time I was ten, I had brought to the register everything from Albert Camus's *The Plague* to pulp novelizations of *The Invaders* TV show. I was a perverse polymorph, devouring books without discrimination or discernment.

My reputation as a serious boy, combined with my eclectic literary tastes, gave me perfect invisibility in the bookstore. At closing time, the employees sometimes almost forgot I was in the store. I'd become part of the furniture, and no one was ever surprised to find me sitting behind the shelves, rummaging through the returns bins, or lurking in the back, poring over dusty stamp-collection display stands.

"Oh, it's you!" the staffer who discovered me in a corner would say before beating an embarrassed retreat, as if I owned the place. This free and easy access, combined with my perennial shortage of pocket money, drove me to crime. It wasn't that my parents would have minded buying me books. The problem was that I devoured them in such quantity every day that it would have cost them a fortune.

Without realizing it, I was rediscovering the basic principle set out by Proudhon and his followers in the nineteenth century: property is theft. The bookseller was a thief, and I, by stealing, was merely exercising my right to property. Better yet: to each according to his needs . . . How right those people were, speaking to me across the centuries, justifying my difficult struggle toward literature! Their protective shadow hovered over me as I crouched behind a bookcase, slipping into my school bag a Mickey Mouse comic book, an issue of *Ciné-Revue* magazine, and the first volume of *Les misérables*.

My visits to the bookstore were so frequent that I knew exactly when the various shipments arrived. One Saturday afternoon I found among the new arrivals a big volume of about twenty *Spirou* magazines bound in a red cloth cover. When I opened the heavy book, it gave off an irresistible aroma. Every page exuded the smell of paper and printing ink too long confined. I felt transported. My throat became dry, my legs weak. A dull excitement gripped my belly. If puberty hadn't been so far in my future, I would have ejaculated right there in the store.

But I'd made it a rule never to steal on Saturdays, and besides, the place was jammed. So, with great effort I closed the magical book, put it back on the shelf, and went home. I spent the rest of the weekend in a daze, my mind completely focused on the feel of the binding, on the matchless discovery the book represented. I had absolutely no need to own the *Spirou* book; my father bought the magazine every week like clockwork. But the idea that comic books could be collected and graced with a hardcover binding for posterity was a revelation at least as staggering as the book itself. Somewhere in the nebulous world of publishing—whose workings I didn't know but which I imagined to be powerful, vast, and labyrinthine— was a man or group of men who had decided to bind a volume of *Spirou*. It was like a sign addressed directly to me, a sign that my tastes and desires were secretly being taken into account. This book was clearly destined for me. I just needed to help set it free.

It would be risky, though. The volume was much larger than any I had stolen up until then, and it was displayed in full view of the entire store. All that Sunday I hatched plans, in my mind making the trip from the door to the display case and back to the door again and again. The mission seemed impossible, and when Monday morning came, I still hadn't found a way out of my dilemma. Then, in the course of the day, I began to glimpse a solution. Since the theft would be impossible during the hours I usually haunted the bookstore, I had to forget all my previous experience and attempt the operation during the slow hours right after the bookstore reopened for the afternoon. That approach, however, posed a related problem. The lycée's discipline was fairly relaxed, but my parents' was not: I was not allowed to leave the school during the day. I would have to skip lunch in the cafeteria at noon, slip out of the lycée without being seen, and get back before 2:00 PM, when my classes resumed. Provided I didn't waste time along the way, it could be done.

If I'd taken some time to review my plan, I would have detected its flaws and weaknesses, but I was so obsessed by that book, I wasn't thinking clearly.

The lunch bell rang. I headed toward the cafeteria with my classmates, then slipped away to hide in the bathrooms. When I stepped out into the school courtyard ten minutes later, I realized that I had broken a school rule for the first time since starting junior high. Thrilled by this victory over myself and my submission, I decided to go out by the main gate, which meant I had to cross the paved courtyard in front of the administrative buildings, where I took a perverse pleasure in pausing by the goldfish pond built in the time of Louis XIV. No one paid any attention to me. When I reached the bus stop, the number 169 was laboring up the hill from Sèvres. I hailed it, climbed on board, and had my ticket punched. My fellow passengers were lost in their thoughts, unaware that they were witnessing the prelude to a major heist to be executed on instinct alone, a high-wire act without a net.

I got off at Bellevue, walked to the bookstore, and got my first shock of disappointment: on Mondays, the store reopened only at 1:45 PM. I felt sick. All that work, all that preparation, for nothing . . . I pressed my face against the window, peering into the shadows. I could make out the display case, the shelf, even the shape of the book. I turned on my heel and walked down a deserted alleyway. I needed to think. I couldn't stay on the main street for long, or I might be spotted by a member of my family at a time when I was supposed to be at school. And if I waited for 1:45, I would only have a few minutes to do the deed before racing back to the lycée.

I decided to let fate settle the matter. I would check the schedule of buses heading back to Sèvres. If a 169 was due at the stop across the street between 1:50 and 1:55, I would make the attempt. Otherwise, I would forget about it. The posted schedule read 1:54. The bus reached the lycée at 2:01. With a final sprint, I could just make it back to class on time.

The book was so heavy, my school bag was sagging. As I climbed our steps that afternoon, I had just one thought: to get rid of it. I rang the bell, and our maid, Madame

Germain, opened the door. She was a large, red-cheeked woman, who intimidated me because she had lost her husband to cancer under awful circumstances. I ran to drop off my school bag in my room, then joined her in the kitchen for tea.

"So, did you have a good day?" she asked, while wiping the sink.

My mouth full, I muttered something in the affirmative.

"Did you treat yourself to a little walk?" she continued in a knowing tone.

I stopped chewing. Madame Germain went on with her housework imperturbably.

"A walk? Oh, no."

She turned around and shook her head.

"Listen, Christian. Don't tell me stories. I saw you at noon."

"That's a surprise. I was at the lycée. It must've been someone else."

She looked dubious, and her eyebrows quivered.

"I may be old, you know, but I'm not crazy!"

For just a moment, I hesitated. What exactly could she have seen? She hadn't mentioned the theft, and I'm sure no one had witnessed it. But what if she'd seen me coming out of the bookstore? If I persisted in my denials, I might be able to shake her certainty, in case she had only glimpsed me. But if she'd actually recognized me, wouldn't lying risk turning her against me, and lead her to tell my parents everything? It had been a trying day, and I didn't have the energy to come up with an imaginative lie.

"Yes, it's true. I left the lycée grounds this afternoon."

Say as little as possible. Don't give her any details she doesn't already have.

"I knew it!" she said triumphantly. "I'm not nearsighted. I glimpsed you from the back, running."

I should have lied! She was bluffing! The old goat got me!

"I just went out for a stroll. You won't say anything, will you? Otherwise, I'll get in trouble."

"You know I don't like tattletales, grown-ups or children. You don't need to worry."

"You won't tell anyone?"

"Of course not. Your parents won't hear about it from me. I just mentioned it to your brother when he came back from school."

She must've seen me turn pale, because she added, "Oh, don't look like that! Daniel won't snitch on you!"

She immediately realized that I didn't share her optimism. My brother Daniel, who was two years younger than me, went to the local public school. Because we weren't allowed to play in the street or vacant lots, he and I were stuck at home a great deal, sharing the same room and the same games. Over the years this enforced proximity had created a powerful history, replete with complicity but also a thousand subtle rivalries and long-held grudges. For example, it was always recognized within the family that of the two of us, I was the genius. Thanks to my brilliant studies and glowing academic career—including skipping a grade—I had outdistanced my brother in the complex geography of classes and school sections. Confirmed by my admiring parents and the long list of *prix d'honneur* and *prix d'excellence* that I effortlessly collected every year, I watched condescendingly as Daniel climbed the rungs of the school ladder. He was among the top ten in his class, which was perfectly respectable, but he couldn't compete with me. This had created a feeling of inferiority that gnawed at him, and which my playing the bookish young scholar only sharpened. For my part, I felt nothing but contempt for his success at sports, especially because I skipped gym class every time I could.

So the revelation of my escapade was a godsend for Daniel, and I knew he had no reason to pass it up.

"He won't say anything, you'll see," said Madame Germain.

I felt defeated, tense with anxiety. If Daniel told my parents that I'd played hooky, and if one of them found the hidden *Spirou* volume, I would be trapped like a rat. Trying to reassure me, Madame Germain followed me into the bedroom, where she made Daniel promise not to say anything. I didn't dare ask him myself, for fear of revealing the extent of the hold he now had over me. He casually agreed, seeming more preoccupied with coloring a map than by our attempt to win him over.

That evening, I sat slumped at my desk, reading and rereading the next day's homework without seeing it. I had stashed the stolen book behind the furniture, but the way my luck was running, someone was sure to find it before the day was over.

The bell rang in the entryway, and Madame Germain went to open the door. Glued to my chair, the very picture of a hard-working boy absorbed in his homework, I strained to hear. My mother exchanged small talk with the maid, and wished her a good night. The door closed.

Silence followed—a long silence. Daniel had left the room while my back was turned, but I tried to convince myself that it was only to go give my mother a kiss.

When she appeared in the doorway, I could tell that she knew.

I tried to deny it, to say that Madame Germain had made a mistake, that she'd even admitted her error. This was my brother's chance to really pour it on by saying that we had tried to get him to keep quiet. During the entire chewing-out that followed, I watched him sitting, perched on his stool, savoring every angry word. When my father came home, my situation became catastrophic. He had stopped by the bakery and the bookstore on his way home from the office, and the bookseller had told him that she'd seen me early in the afternoon shortly before there had been a theft from the display case. She couldn't swear that I was responsible, but she remembered seeing me several times in the back of the store, talking with a boy who had a bad reputation, and she was afraid I'd been put up to it.

Now I started getting it from both sides. On one side was my mother, distressed at the idea that I could have disobeyed her and, which was worse, was spending my days hanging out with street punks. On the other was my father, who prized honesty above all other virtues, mortified at the idea that I might be guilty of stealing. I was terrified. Not only didn't I want to admit the theft, I couldn't. One thing would lead to another, and I knew that a confession would lead to a search of my desk and my bookshelves, where a slew of stolen books and magazines stood hidden behind a neat facade of comic books.

I persisted in denying that I'd met with somebody in the bookstore. I didn't belong to a gang; I hadn't been blackmailed or manipulated. In fact, I had no idea what my parents were talking about.

"I can go see the bookseller and talk to her, if you like. She'll realize she made a mistake."

"The bookseller made a mistake! Madame Germain made a mistake! Do you think we're idiots?"

Dismayed, I tried to think through the consequences of a partial confession. I realized that Madame Germain would be grilled as soon as she came tomorrow morning. She would play for time and try to protect me, as she had promised. But since my brother had already ratted on me, she couldn't stay on that tack for long without risking her job. She would eventually admit she had glimpsed me on the street, and would get off with a lecture. Under the circumstances, it was in my interest to lower the pressure a notch by at least admitting my escapade, while denying any participation in a theft at the bookstore, particularly since the flaw in the bookseller's claim—the hypothetical meeting with a thug between rows of Roger Martin du Gard and Henri Troyat—had never taken place. On that point, at least, my stance of offended innocence was still fairly credible.

I therefore confessed to leaving the lycée grounds and promised never to do so again. A punishment was decided on—I would be deprived of my constitutional right to a weekly franc—and I submitted with good grace, delighted to get off so lightly. Our parents finally left the bedroom, but not until my father grabbed me by the shoulders and finished me off by murmuring, "It's better when you tell the truth, isn't it? You feel cleaner." This plunged me into an abyss of shame and terror. Shame at what I was and terror at the idea that my parents could be fooled so easily.

My brother and I found ourselves in the bedroom, facing each other. He had a snarky little smile on his face. I wanted to kill him.

I had been the perfect student, the most loathsome teacher's pet produced by the French educational system since the dismissal of Maréchal Pétain. Up to now I'd spent all my school time sitting in the front row, my eyes locked on the teacher with the soft, moist gaze of a faithful Labrador retriever. But the moment I started junior high in an "international section"—one of the rare pedagogical experiments of the time—I sensed the mood of permissiveness set by the more revolutionary of our teachers, and decided to take full advantage of it. Faced with a baffled and hesitant administration, these men and women created within the lycée an idyllic community where we could give free rein to our imaginations in a cacophony worthy of the Tower of Babel. In the course of the semesters they introduced us to expressive movement, photography, and film, while the regular lycée students, or "normals" as we contemptuously dubbed them, were stuck with math quizzes and science homework.

But I was stuck with my brother.

And course my parents found the books.

"Whatever are we going to do about you? What are we going to do?" repeated my mother to no one in particular.

Devastated by the knowledge that his son was a thief,

my father was long past saying anything. He had taken an enormous shipping carton from the closet where he stored his hand tools and fix-it supplies, and was filling it with the books and magazines. At first, he'd allowed me to quickly examine each one, giving me time to separate the honestly acquired ones from the fruits of my delinquency. But as I glumly muttered "bought" or "stolen," a coincidence occurred to me that felt almost overwhelmingly obscene. A few weeks earlier, I had read Simon Wiesenthal's *Murderers Among Us,* a book that changed my life. This grotesque book selection reminded me— though I couldn't grasp the enormity of the comparison I was unconsciously making—of the selection process of the deportees on their arrival at Auschwitz, as survivors later reported: *"Links, rechts, links, links, rechts . . .* Left, right, left, left, right . . ."

My father eventually wearied of this incongruous selection and started tossing the tomes littering my bed into the box pell-mell. "The bookseller paid for all these books. She didn't steal them." When the bed was cleared, he closed the carton, lifted it with difficulty (its weight made him grunt with weariness and disgust), and set it down in his closet. It remained there for years, untouched by human hands, a mute monument to my familial disgrace.

Translated by William Rodarmor

—{ Roissy }—

Down in the Dumps
at Charles de Gaulle Airport

Frédéric Beigbeder

WARNING. In the 1980s a new drug appeared in the nightspots: MDMA, otherwise known as Ecstasy. This "love potion" had some strange effects: hot flashes, techno nights, anonymous embraces, teeth grinding, rapid dehydration, existential angst, suicide attempts, and marriage proposals. It was a hard drug with highs and lows as steep as a roller coaster or an American thriller. The author of this short story has stopped taking it and advises the reader not to start. Not only is Ecstasy illegal, but it rots the brain, as this story, written under its influence, makes clear. And anyway, do we really need to take a pill so we can tell our life story to complete strangers? We have literature for that. —*F. B.*

FRÉDÉRIC BEIGBEDER (1965–) is a bad-boy writer and pundit whose surface frivolity hides a trenchant social observer that can be both provocative and self-critical. "When I have a cold, people think I've been snorting drugs," he says. "That's called having a reputation." This story is from Beigbeder's 1999 collection, *Nouvelles sous ecstasy*.

Didyalike it? Didya? Didya? Didyalikeit? Who are you? Why are we talking with our faces just inches apart? Is it true that you read my latest book? Can you guarantee that I'm not *dreaming*? Is it possible to have such a pretty red mouth? Is it *reasonable* to be so cute, to be twenty-one and wear a size XXXS T-shirt? Do you realize the risk you're taking by paying me a compliment with such blue eyes?

Why is my hand sweating in yours? Why do your knees make me want to invent transitive verbs? What time is it, anyway? What's your name? Will you marry me? Can you tell me where we are right now? What's that gumdrop you just put on our tongues? Why are those laser beams slicing through a layer of liquid oxygen? Who are those magnums of champagne whistling over our heads for? How soon do we regret being born? You have beautiful eyes, you know that? Why are you crying? When will you kiss me? Would you like another vodka? When are we going to kiss again? Why have you stopped dancing? Who are all these people—your friends or my enemies? Would you take off your sweater, please? How many children do you want? What are your favorite kids' names?

What should we do now? Want to go out and get some air? Are we already outside? Shall we call a taxi? Your place or mine? You'd rather walk? Why should we go up the Champs-Élysées? Is it really such a good idea to take our shoes off to walk on the pavement? Can you heat a teaspoon over the flame at the Tomb of the Unknown Soldier? Do you have a boyfriend? Why am I thinking the same things you're thinking? Do you know many people who say the exact same thing at the same time? Why is that cop staring at us? Why are all those cars going round the Arc de Triomphe? Why don't they go home? What about us? Why don't we go home? How long are we going to sit here on the Place de l'Étoile, giving each other sloppy kisses in subzero temperatures instead of making love in a bed like everyone else?

Do you think it was a good idea to steal that cop's kepi? Are you sure the police can't run as fast as we can? Does this motorbike belong to you? You sure you can drive in this condition? Can't you slow down? Why take the expressway? Is it really a good idea to lean so far into the turns at 180 kilometers an hour? Is it legal to zigzag between trucks at six o'clock in the morning? Will the sun rise tomorrow? Why go to Roissy–Charles de Gaulle Airport? Does life change when you change cities? What's the point of traveling in a world where everything's the same? Aren't you cold? Am I the only one freezing my nuts off? What? Can't you hear anything I say because of your helmet? So I can shout whatever I want? I could sing, "I wanna hold your hand?" I could go on lying to you while I stroke your back under your sweater, then your breasts under your bra, then my fingers in your panties, shit, would that make you slow down?

Where are we going to park this thing? In front of Terminal 1 or in the parking lot? Why is this parking space labeled 4NC8? Looks like "fornicate," doesn't it? How long does this pill last? Why do automatic doors open before you touch them? Why do those pale neon lights make us feel like we're skipping around on the moon? Are we really taking twenty-foot leaps or is that an illusion? Could you start kissing me again? Would you mind if I came in your mouth? Would it be okay if we lock ourselves in the bathroom so I can fuck your face? Will you swallow me if I lick your pussy?

Was it good? Was it really, really good? Jesus, it was absolutely terrific, but what time is it? Why must night *always* be followed by day? Instead of walking backward on the moving sidewalks inside fat Plexiglas tubes—a tangle of pipes built in the seventies that look like the ventilator tubes they shove down accident victims' throats—huh? I was saying, instead of screwing around in Roissy, why don't we take a plane? The first one out of here? Anywhere but here? So that the adventure never ends? Fly off to Venezuela or Belorussia or Sri Lanka or Vietnam? Where the sun is setting? Can you see the letters clicking on the old-fashioned departures board: Dublin? Cologne? Oran? Tokyo? Shanghai? Amsterdam? Madrid? Edinburgh? Colombo? Oslo? Berlin? Is every city a question? Do you miss the planes after they take off at the end of the runway? Do you know that there are blue stewardesses on board, serving the first plastic-wrapped meal trays to businessmen on Valium? Can you hear the departure information intoned in a flat, colorless voice by a sad hostess after the electronic jingle? Can I caress your lips some more before we go home? Which of us will leave first? Why oh whyyyy must we say goodbyyye?

Do airports depress you as much as they do me? Don't you think there's a kind of poetry in these places at cross-roads? A melancholy in departures? A lyricism in reunions? An atmospheric density laden with air-conditioned emotions? How long does the descent take? Will our love survive without chemical vacations? When will we stop being silent as we watch the dawn come up over this empty cafeteria? Why do all the newsstands stay closed and the video games remain blank? Do you envy those middle managers waiting for their flights in linoleum-floored lounges, sprawled on orange couches, drinking instant coffee? What is there to say about that customs officer with halitosis, that janitor dragging that noisy garbage can on wheels, those homeless people snoring away on the mauve plastic benches? What are they trying to tell us? That escape is impossible? That we can never get away from ourselves? That journeys lead nowhere? That you must be on vacation for your whole life or else not at all? Could you let go of my hand, please? Can't you see I need to be alone among all these abandoned suitcases? Could we go our separate ways without too much pain, even in front of the Gucci ad for Envy?

And as we watched the 747s take off, our eyes moist, I was still wondering, Why aren't we on board?

Translated by Anna Livia

Vanity

Cyrille Fleischman

THE ONLY REAL REMEMBRANCE Simon Kéversak left to his friends and family was the cold almost all of them caught at the Bagneux Cemetery.

And so, at the headstone unveiling—about a year after the burial, in keeping with tradition—there wasn't much of a crowd. Many people had been notified, of course, either by the secretary of the association Kéversak had belonged to, or through the Yiddish newspaper. But very few made the trip.

Kéversak, who had neither wife nor children, had bought his plot before he died and had taken care of all

CYRILLE FLEISCHMAN (1941–) has managed to create a shtetl of the mind in the heart of the Marais neighborhood of Paris, drawing from the same well of Jewish irony, wit, and fantasy as Sholem Aleichem and I. B. Singer. In addition to his popular *Métro Saint-Paul* trilogy, his books include *L'attraction du bal* (1987), *Juste une petite valse* (2000), and *Une rencontre loin de l'Hôtel de Ville* (2004). In 2002, Fleischman won the Max Cukierman Yiddish Culture Award for his body of work. This story appears in Fleischman's 1992 collection, *Rendez-vous au métro Saint-Paul*.

the details. He had even drafted the inscription for the stone. In his will he had bequeathed his estate to the association, so its president, treasurer, and secretary were there, as well as a man who'd arrived early for another ceremony. Plus a former salesclerk of Kéversak's who'd missed the funeral but came for the unveiling out of a sense of guilt.

Everyone was wondering what the supposed ceremony would be like: they didn't have the ten people needed to say Kaddish; it was even colder than it had been the year before; the inscription on the headstone was covered with snow; and the president, who was to give a speech, had forgotten the piece of paper on which he'd jotted a few notes. The five men standing next to the mortuary representative were stamping their feet to keep warm.

"So, shall we begin?" the secretary asked.

"Begin *what*?" the president replied. "I say we all go for coffee at the café across from the main entrance, so we can warm up. We came. We saw. We paid our respects to poor old Simon. That's enough already in this kind of weather."

The others agreed, except for the mortuary assistant, who didn't want to take sides, though he would have appreciated a kind word about the quality of the marble and the inscription. With a gloved hand, he nonchalantly brushed away the fine layer of snow. The gold letters against the black stone were indeed handsomely inscribed. The president cast a distracted glance at them.

He was about to join the four men already leaving that section of the cemetery when he stopped and spun around to confirm what he'd glimpsed. Dumbfounded, he called out to the others, who had continued on their way. The secretary retraced his steps and was soon followed by the other three. They all looked at the inscription on the marble the president was pointing at. The secretary read out loud: "Simon Kéversak, 1918–1978, Honorary President of the Association of Small Specialty Shopkeepers Hailing from Kraków and Who Lived in Montreuil before the War."

The first and last names, the dates, and the association's title were all correct—but Kéversak had never been president, much less honorary president. He'd never even managed to get elected himself treasurer. The secretary turned to the mortuary assistant.

"You're sure you didn't make a mistake on the stone?"

"I beg your pardon? Did the marble cutter get the dates wrong?"

"Not the dates," the president interjected. "But what comes after. He was never the president of our group."

The assistant looked at the inscription, pulled a piece of paper from his pocket, and compared the two.

"Everything is correct. The notary wrote us with this inscription."

"What notary? You need a notary to put a name on a stone?" the president asked, exasperated.

The assistant grew uncomfortable. The others even more so.

Who was there to complain to? Kéversak's whole family was dead. That left only the notary, but would they really go bother a notary in the depths of winter on account of some dead idiot's fantasy?

The president grabbed the mortuary assistant by the arm and led him off.

The others followed, and everyone wound up on the main path, which was covered with snow.

The former salesclerk, who'd kept silent until then, caught up with the president and the mortuary worker.

"Excuse me, but I overheard what you were saying. I used to be a salesclerk for Monsieur Simon when he had his shop. He always talked about your society, and he was very proud of being *someone* among you."

The president released the mortuary assistant, who in any case understood nothing of the problem, and turned to the little red-haired fellow, who really had no business butting in.

"He was *not* someone! He was nobody at all, except an active member who was three years late with his dues!"

The salesclerk persisted. "Yes, but he left you his entire fortune!"

The others, seeing that they'd stopped in the snow to argue, came to join them. The treasurer had caught just the last sentence.

"His fortune, his fortune . . . Let's not exaggerate!" he sighed. "Once all his debts were paid off, there was no more left than would have bought a crocodile purse for his wife, if he'd had a wife. That's all there was in his will!"

"My wife doesn't have a croc skin purse," the salesclerk retorted. "And Monsieur Simon always told me that since he had no family, he would leave me something. Thirty years I worked for him. He didn't leave me a thing."

The president, who was freezing cold, bridled at that remark. "So we're here to talk about your wife's purse?"

They started walking again, firmly this time, toward the exit. They went up the little walkway along the right-hand fence and continued to the main entrance. Across from the café. The café where people would stop for a glass of wine after leaving the cemetery, to prove to themselves they weren't in Bagneux for good. The president crossed the street first. The others, following him, entered the well-heated room, and flumped down at a table.

While they were ordering—a café au lait for each, plus a croissant for the president—the little salesclerk tried to convince the mortuary worker that his former boss had been unfair to him. On the other side of the table, the treasurer, the secretary, and their unexpected colleague— the one who'd come for another ceremony and was still early—were expounding great truths in matters of life, death, cold, vacation . . . in short, everything that can be said while sitting in a café across from the Bagneux Cemetery in winter.

Only the president was silent. This inscription business stuck in his craw.

"And if we were to name him anyway?" he suddenly blurted out.

"What do you mean?" the secretary asked.

"I'm wondering, shouldn't we name Simon Kéversak honorary president?"

"But he's *dead*," the treasurer stressed.

The president twitched. "No, he's alive, but he prefers to stay in a vault so he won't get wet in the snow . . . Of course he's dead!"

"Don't get upset!" said the secretary. "What exactly are you trying to say?"

"I was saying," the president continued, "that we should name him honorary president. That way there wouldn't be a lie on his headstone. And what's it to us, after all? We've never had an honorary president. We can simply start with him."

Then the fourth man, the one who'd come early for another funeral, stood up. "Excuse me, but it's time for my cousin's funeral. I can already see the whole family across the street. If the snow doesn't delay the procession, it should be here any minute. Good-bye, and may we meet again in happier times!"

He laid a coin on the table to pay for his order and was about to leave when he had another thought. "You know, I enjoyed being with all of you for the ceremony just now. How fortuitous to have two things to do in Bagneux on the same day! But I've been thinking, it doesn't seem right for you to name Kéversak honorary president. Oh well, do whatever you like."

And he left.

The mortuary worker got up next to go have a glass of red wine at the counter; he couldn't stand café au lait. The others were now alone at the table, and the president continued with his thoughts. "On the one hand, it's true that it's not right to name Simon honorary president; on the other hand, it would nonetheless be better for the inscription; but on the *other* hand . . . "

The secretary cut in. "Excuse me, but what if we just name him honorary treasurer? That's only one word to change. We could ask the marble cutter to do it."

"Are you crazy, or what?" said the treasurer, nearly choking. "Honorary treasurer for a guy who ran against me ten times and never got elected because everyone knew he was a nut? If you do that, I'm handing in my resignation. Why not honorary secretary, for that matter?"

The secretary looked up at the ceiling, as if the other man had said something outrageous.

Kéversak's former salesclerk reentered the fray. "Listen, you guys aren't fair in your society! If I'd gotten something in his will, I'd gladly have made Monsieur Simon my honorary boss. Head honorary boss, even, if that would please a dead man!"

The president wasn't listening. He stood up. "I must take another look at the stone!"

"We'll go with you," the secretary and the treasurer both said at once.

The president placed a bill on the table to pay for their orders, and they went outside. It had started to snow again.

They looked at the procession forming on the main path. It was probably the funeral that the other association member had come for.

The three men, followed a few feet behind by the little redheaded salesclerk, who didn't want to leave them, turned left and walked toward the section where Kéversak was buried. The mortuary worker had stayed behind at the café counter, so only the four of them left footprints in the fresh snow. By the time they were standing in front of Simon Kéversak's tomb, the inscription was once again covered in white. The president wiped the new marble with the sleeve of his overcoat. "We shall be going home shortly, but he's here for good." He hesitated. "It's quite sad, really, death . . . "

The treasurer was slapping his hands. He was cold. The wind blew snow into their faces under their hats. "You're not going to give the speech now, are you?" he asked worriedly. "We'll all catch cold for nothing. No offense; I'm saying it for your sake: look how it's coming down! You've already got snow all over your hat."

Indeed, snowflakes clung to the president's overcoat and his brown fedora.

"He was unlucky, poor old Simon . . . We really ought to do something," the president said. He was speaking more to himself than to the others, but the snow was swirling steadily. The secretary tugged at his sleeve. "We're leaving now."

One after another they left the section. When they reached the path, the president stopped in his tracks. "I've decided: Simon Kéversak *will* be honorary president—on the inscription. And only there. That way, everything is in order."

The others, glad to be going, said nothing more. They hastened toward the main gate of the cemetery. The ceremony was over. They had the feeling they'd been more conscientious than they might have expected.

Simon Kéversak would have been pleased, they concluded as they parted ways.

But there where he was, it all merely left him cold.

Translated by Rose Vekony

An Ear for an Ear

Samuel Benchetrit

KARIM AND DANIEL once went to the annual party of the Communist newspaper *L'Humanité*, but they sure didn't go for the sake of humanity. They went to pick up girls, or to nicely beat up the boyfriends of the girls who turned them down. Daniel was a real public menace in those days because a guy from T Tower had taught him the ear-tearing technique. The phrase may seem mysterious, but it means exactly what it says: ear-tearing = ripping off a human ear.

To do it, you have to be fast: the move consists in grabbing the upper part of the ear between your thumb and index finger, squeezing hard, and giving a sharp, decisive yank. When the guy sees someone holding his ear in

---

SAMUEL BENCHETRIT (1973–) is a writer, actor, and movie director who grew up in the housing projects outside Paris. Born into a family of modest means, he quit school at fifteen to work at a series of small jobs, including photographer's assistant and movie theater usher. After writing *Récit d'un branleur* (2000), a provocative first novel, he started a five-volume portrait of his neighborhood, *Chroniques de l'asphalte*. This story is from the first volume, *Le temps des tours* (2005).

his hand, he usually has no idea what happened. Daniel tended to rub it in, threatening to feed this little piece of you to his dog, Marley (Bob), an easygoing German shepherd who would calmly watch the blood streaming down your head.

The situation created some incongruous dialogue.

"Give me back my ear, please."

"Please don't feed my ear to your dog!"

"What's my mother gonna say when I come home without my ear?"

On the day of the party, Karim and Daniel got up early (1:45 PM) to take the RER train to La Courneuve.

If you wanted to pick up girls at the *L'Humanité* party, you had to get there early. Like Disneyland, to avoid the lines. And that day, there were millions of Karims and Daniels. Impossible to find a girl who didn't have ten guys around her, all waiting to try their luck once she'd shot you down.

Still, they did manage to spend some time with a couple of girls.

The first was a certain Valérie, who tried to give Karim a Communist Youth membership card.

A sad, short story that ended this way.

"Sure you don't want your C. Y. card?"

"Sure you don't want your fat bitch card?"

Then there was the very gloomy Marie-Chantal, who shared her thoughts about anarchy with Daniel.

"The world's on the wrong track, see, everything's virtual. We're living in a big video game, and I don't want to be the main character. All my life people have wanted me to believe in supposedly solid institutions that were good for me. But now that I've discovered anarchy, the more they want to believe in it—well, the less I do."

"You've got nice tits."

"What?"

Finally Karim and Daniel went to a concert by Rêve Sanglant, five burned-out guys who were depressed about everything and moved in slow motion.

The lead singer came on stage, and instead of just saying to the audience, "Hi, how are you?" he said: "I've got some good news for you. You're all gonna die."

Karim didn't much like people talking to him like that.

"Why's that asshole telling me this?"

"Forget it. It's a singer thing."

The first song was called "Canigou," and its main point was to compare us to the canine species.

SINGER:
  You listen to them talk about their political dreams
  And you . . .
BACKUP SINGERS:
  Shake hands, shake hands.
SINGER:
  You're nothing but a pawn on their big chessboard
  And you . . .
BACKUP SINGERS:
  Sit up and beg, sit up and beg.

The crowd began to respond, but Karim and Daniel just stood there. They couldn't understand why the singer was insulting them, much less why the crowd was dancing instead of weeping.

If Karim and Daniel had left before the chorus, none of the rest of this story would've happened. But they stayed, unfortunately, and heard this:

[Chorus]
SINGER:
   We're all dogs.
SINGER AND BACKUP SINGERS:
   Your brother's a dog,
   Your sister's a bitch,
   Your father's a dog,
   Your mother's a bitch.

Karim put his hand in his pocket and absentmindedly released his switchblade's safety catch. Daniel started to seriously check out the singer's ears.

Just to be sure, Karim asked, "What's he saying there?"

"That your mother's a bitch."

"Damn, what an asshole! Come on!"

My two friends slipped backstage to wait for the singer and his band, who had no idea that a six-foot-three-inch guy who could handle a knife like nobody's business and a quick little ear-ripper were waiting to kill them.

After an hour and a half of ranting, Rêve Sanglant left the stage, with people who wanted to be insulted some more still shouting, "One more song! One more song! One more song!"

Karim walked up to the singer.

"You calling my mother a bitch?"

"What?"

"You said my mother and my whole family were dogs."

"I didn't say your mother was a bitch. Well, not your mother particularly. All mothers, even mine."

"Even your mother? Damn, don't you have any self-respect?"

"No, no, it's just a metaphor."

Karim turned to Daniel.

"What's he saying?"

"A metaphor. That girl who doesn't believe in anything said something like that before. They're trying to confuse us."

"I'll show you a metaphor!"

At that, Karim discreetly opened his switchblade and jabbed it into the singer's leg, who fell to his knees.

"That's for my mother."

Then he kneed him full in the face, smashing his nose.

"And that's for yours."

Daniel, an energetic sort who didn't like wasting time, went over to yank the lead guitar player's ear. He was especially annoyed because the guy had smashed his guitar on an amplifier.

"Aren't you ashamed at breaking your guitar? Don't you think it'd be better to give it to some kid who doesn't have the money to buy one?"

"I couldn't care less, 'cause people give me my axes. Anyway, who are you to be telling me what to do?"

Zip! No left ear.

There weren't any encores that evening.

As they left, Karim and Daniel passed a truck full of musical instruments. Daniel remembered what the guitar player had told him, and mentioned it to Karim.

"People give them their instruments, you know."

"What do you mean?"

"Like, they get their gear for free. That's why they break that stuff. It doesn't cost them anything."

Karim thought hard for a moment, but Daniel was the first to speak.

"Let's just take it. May as well sell the gear instead of their smashing it."

"Exactly what I was thinking."

"You know how to drive a truck?"

"When you can drive my father's R20, you can drive anything."

Nine guitars. Four basses. Two drum sets. All sorts of percussion. Seven mics with stands. A violin, even.

Karim and Daniel stashed the stuff in a couple of the tower's empty basements, and quickly let it be known they had instruments for sale.

I belonged to the gang, so I was among the first to get the word. Daniel showed me the instruments with the enthusiasm of a Stradivarius maker.

I chose a guitar. I didn't know what I was doing, so I selected it by color and shape. It was white and looked new, but I especially liked that it looked like one Keith Richards played.

Olivier Berthot, fifth floor, bought a bass. William Foré, a local punk who sang with the Death Dogs and lived on the eleventh, took a drum set and some percussion pieces. Véronique Almeida, fourth floor, bought herself a bass to please Pierro Gonzalez on the fifteenth, who acquired a guitar. Monsieur Touré, thirteenth floor, happily bought a guitar for his son Boubou, eleven, a bass for his son Henry, ten, and a drum set for his youngest, Benjamin, nine.

"Like the Jackson Five!"

"But there's only three of them!"

"So much the better. We'll call them the Jackson Three."

Finally Madame Prévost, a retired French teacher on the tenth floor, overcame five minutes of embarrassment, went down to the basement, and paid Karim the five hundred francs he wanted for the violin.

(The amps and mics were premiums Karim and Daniel gave with every purchase of an instrument.)

The merchandise moved in less than a month for a little over thirty thousand francs, which Karim and Daniel invested in soft drugs.

Nearly all the tower inhabitants now had an instrument, but nobody knew how to play them.

A friend once told me this: "There are two kinds of people. The ones who speak English well but don't dare speak it even in England, and the ones who don't speak it at all but use English even in France."

That pretty well summed up what happened in the tower over the following weeks. The people used their respective instruments so confidently that the tower turned into a huge, pain-wracked organ, which seemed to be convulsing and shrieking in agony.

Cacophony reigned as the tower dwellers battled each other with wah-wah pedals and endless drum rolls. And unless Madame Prévost was strangling a cat, she was playing her violin.

For my part, I tirelessly tried to play Bob Marley's "Redemption Song," first on the guitar, then on the bass I got from Véronique Almeida because Pierro Gonzalez wasn't interested in her.

After a while, the racket gradually died down. Monsieur Touré threatened to kill the Jackson Three if they continued to act like the Jackson Five. The Death Dogs split up. Madame Prévost went back to poetry.

Each morning, you'd find another instrument in the garbage. Karim and Daniel briefly considered retrieving them and selling them in a neighboring project, but once they thought it over, they decided to stick to the soft drug business.

Translated by William Rodarmor

Dog Mind
Luc Lang

. . . IT'S TRUE! I'm not indifferent to my neighbor's charms, but she puts up such a front of respectability, a businesswoman, nicely turned out, elegant to her fingertips, runs her life with an iron fist in an astrakhan glove . . . secretary to the chief executive, she says, eighteen years as the personal assistant to the CEO of BP France, guardian of the temple on the top floor of a skyscraper in La Défense, a multinational company's memory bank from 1987 to 2005 . . . when the CEO hung up his gloves, she handed in her apron and took early retirement, probably with a slew of stock options. We're within a few years of being in the same age bracket, in our fifties, both athletic,

LUC LANG (1956–) is a prizewinning novelist whose books include *Voyage sur la ligne d'horizon* (1988), *Liverpool Marée Haute* (1991), *Mille six cents ventres* (1998, tr. *Strange Ways*), *Les Indiens* (2001), *11 septembre, mon amour* (2003), and *La fin des paysages* (2006). Lang often immerses himself in the milieus he writes about: jazz musicians, ambulance drivers, power linemen, and neurosurgeons. He teaches esthetics at the Ecole nationale supérieure des Beaux-Arts de Cergy, and is a frequent guest at writers' conferences in the United States.

we'd be a very presentable couple, no, I mean it! it would
be easy, we live in adjoining houses, just knock down the
dividing walls . . . but she also owns a huge peach orchard
in back that she has let go to ruin, it's off limits even to
her two pedigree hounds, they might pick up ticks in the
weeds . . . what a waste! she prefers to park them like
china dogs out front, on her seventy square yards of English lawn . . . I offered to get the orchard back in shape,
prune, prune the peach trees, replace the dead and dying
ones with cherry and apple, which are tougher and a lot
longer-lived . . . she peers at me, scrutinizes me like an
iris scanner, and finally answers, that's a marvelous idea,
Monsieur Marconi, I'll have to think about it . . . she sus-
pects me of wanting to take over her property with my
two little granddaughters, whom I raise almost single-
handedly with my daughter, an actress who is often on
tour and whose husband took off, just disappeared one
fine day . . . no doubt about it, it would be win-win, she'd
get beautiful fruit and a rejuvenated landscape, and I'd
get some space . . . but she doesn't give a damn about the
fruit or the landscape, all that matters is her territorial
integrity, with a return on investment if possible . . . last
week she spoke approvingly of a suggestion by Monsieur
Darmont, a realtor, to build some thirty enclosed parking
spaces back there, an excellent investment given the parking problem in the neighborhood, you would access them
from Rue Thiers . . . yeah, right! I could already hear the
screeching metal doors, the revving, the rumbling lines
of cars, exhausts fuming, tires churning the gravel from
7:00 AM, not sixty yards from our bedroom windows . . .
she's crazy . . . and it's not as though I hadn't tried to be

friendly, tried to soften her up: Call me Ettore! . . . how many times has that been on the tip of my tongue? Call me Ettore, dear Marie-Laure, and hey! why not, a tumble in the tall grass in the shade of the peach trees, because I must say she's a real turn-on . . . well, screw it! she can keep her drawing-room language and her "dear Monsieur Marconi," that way of creating distance by letting you know how overbooked her life already is, what with her two pets and her bridge games . . . but this thing about thirty-six parking spaces in the peach orchard was the last straw . . . that did it: I got the message loud and clear—and the first target would be her precious Tibetan grey-hounds who (1) bark the moment my little angels Yasmé and Julia start chattering on our miserable scrap of lawn, and (2) howl like crazy all afternoon on the three days a week when Madame Chinon goes off to her girlfriends' for their unspeakable bridge games.

Why target innocent animals? you might ask . . . no idea, a hunch that they might be her Achilles' heel, the chink in her armor . . . anyway, it's her or me, poor fool that I am who got to watch her out walking her living sculptures as if she were parading along the Promenade des Anglais in a *concours d'élégance* . . . the creatures would proceed with Apollonian slowness, looking like an ancient architectural frieze, all muscle and fur, along the Neuilly sidewalks beneath the century-old plane trees of Avenue Maréchal Pétain . . . the dogs' pads meeting the asphalt with all the gravitas of prancing Republican Guard horses . . . and she, with her crow-black blue-highlighted hair, pillbox hat, and white designer suit, holding her living works of art on double red crocodile-skin leashes, betraying not a trace of doubt as to the visual success of the tableau—justifiably so, they certainly made a pretty picture! And when the aforesaid living sculptures take a dump in the gutter (because Azor and Mira are perfectly trained, of course) she basks in obvious, boundless civic pride as she takes up the requisite pose, standing erect, gazing off into the distance, at once involved and detached, her hawk-like nose quivering in the foul effluvia, yes, indeed, a veritable paragon of virtue . . . —but Madame Chinon, if you could just have them do their business a hundred yards or so farther on, our tires wouldn't be plastered with their sticky doo-doo all the time . . . I know, I know, this way the cars actively participate in the dissemination of Azor and Mira's fecal matter, which is all to the good, but the wheels of our cars, bikes, and motorcycles are always getting smeared and our little bike shed stinks to high heaven and . . . —what you're asking of me is very difficult, Monsieur Marconi! the gutter is, well, it's their Eldorado! the poor animals have to go so badly when I take them out, it's quite impossible for them to go farther than across the sidewalk . . . —I don't doubt it, my dear madam, at their first glimpse of the gutter, bingo! the sphincters loosen, the dogs' anuses nearly attain bliss and nirvana . . . her head jerked back, flamingo-like . . . still, maybe it would help to take them out earlier? . . . she makes no reply, shoots me a cosmetic smile, and after bidding me good day hastens off to her bridge group.

My graphic design studio is on the first floor facing the street, and two days later I spotted her frenziedly drag-

ging Azor toward the gutter, but in vain . . . his ears
half erect, eyes staring, expression frozen, paws riveted
to the ground, fully focused on the peristaltic pressure
on his rectum, Azor energetically deposited a large,
barely solidified turd on the sidewalk . . . I saw panic
seize Madame Chinon, her eyes darting left and right,
interrogating the fronts of the nearby houses, but no one
had seen it, whew! and she walked off regally, her two
mutts seeming to head up an honor guard . . . I waited
five minutes, grabbed a can of spray paint from my desk,
went out to the sidewalk, covered the monumental turd
with a thick coat of gold paint, then wrote the caption "I
SAW YOU!" beneath it. I watched from my office window
for her return, she started when she saw the gilded excre-
tion with the accompanying message clearly directed at
her . . . her panicky eyes again darted every which way . . .
the next day, when the city's combat-suited Merde Max
patrolmen roared up on their green pooper-scooper and
brush-vacuumed up Mister Azor's massive bowel movement, what remained behind on the concrete was the
permanent outline of the now-vanished turd, a haunting
reminder of Azor's misdeed and Lady Chinon's lapse . . .
—did you see the graffiti on the sidewalk? . . . —yes, she
answers, that's all I needed . . . —but what does that "I
SAW YOU" mean, Madame Chinon? . . . —how should
I know, Monsieur? . . . her aplomb, her rustproof confidence in her exalted place in the world, again fills my
mouth with the taste of bile . . . all right, on to Stage 2, in
the shape of 20-gram packets of magnesium chloride, but
let me explain: a single packet of powdered magnesium
chloride diluted in a liter of water will totally flush out

both small and large intestine. My ex-wife is a nutrition-
ist, and she made a point of giving us the runs every two
months: rinse out the bowels, eliminate the toxins that so
gravely compromise our immune system, it was a way of
life for her. Getting back to my chloride, I mix the white
powder with some ground meat, roll it into little balls,
and toss these onto the English lawn at Azor and Mira's
feet . . . they love them, beg for more . . . after three days
of meaty treats, a true intestinal uproar begins for them . . .
a week later, the lawn is streaked with acid burns, and
the long ivory-colored hairs on the greyhounds' butts
have changed into a sort of kinky, saffron-colored wool,
early-autumn haloes ringing Azor and Mira's anuses
like bull's-eyes . . . I notice Milady Chinon hanging her
carpets from the windows, her battle against the smelly
stains has begun . . .

Thursday, June 7: she's late for the first time as she
rushes out of the house and trots off to her bridge four-
some, her face tense, terrified of the catastrophe looming
behind her. . . that same day, leaning out of my studio
window, I catch sight of her on her hands and knees with
a mop, scrubbing her lawn as one might scrub a tile floor
—Madame Chinon! nice evening, isn't it? —oh, yes, good
evening —tell me, what are those strange burn marks on
your beautiful lawn? —it's a disease, she mutters, light-
ning attacks of dehydration —couldn't it be pollution, a
toxic radioactive cloud? . . . she shrugs . . . something like
Chernobyl, only on a smaller scale? —you seem to like
the idea of worldwide disaster; and why would this cloud,
as you call it, stop right at the fence line? —oh, there's no
comparison! on my side it isn't even lawn, just a strip of

ordinary grass . . . dead silence, no point in rubbing it in, night-night Marie-Laure, and sweet dreams!

On Friday morning I park in front of the house after dropping my granddaughters off at school and open the car door to find Marie-Laure standing at her garden gate, the two dogs at her feet . . . she tucks one under her arm like a football, sprints across the sidewalk without breaking stride, and tosses it into the gutter, what an athlete! she goes back to get the other one, and one-two! left-right-left, three strides in her pink running shoes, and Azor and Mira have landed in the gutter looking stunned. Marie-Laure is wearing an old pair of pants and a nylon coverall blouse, she is beet-red and trying to catch her breath . . . are you working out, Madame Chinon? . . . she shrugs, the way she did the day before —they're sick! —who? —my greyhounds! they're sick! —them, too? you mean it's a mass poisoning? first the English lawn, then the Nepalese greyhounds —Tibetan! —sorry, I always get mixed up —and both at once, too! like food poisoning, even though their diet is purely organic and vegetarian! the vet has seen them, checked them out, more or less, and they're in perfect health except that they suffer continually from loose stools —which they spread far and wide, I dare say —yes, but what puzzles the vet is that they should both be sick at the same time, and they haven't been eating anything! have you ever heard of such a thing? —are you sure it's not psychosomatic? they're twins, after all, a sort of joint complaint, an interactive depression? . . . she stares at me as if I'm speaking Chinese —haven't you ever read about that kind of thing? —well, yes, perhaps there are studies —I'll find the article for you, don't worry, there's group psychotherapy —stuff and nonsense! —no, no, I'm serious, you have sessions with only the animals, then sessions with the animals and their owners, to recover the primal scream energy, release tensions, untie displaced psychotic knots, get beyond the anal stage —well I suppose, under the circumstances —they say you have to talk to animals a lot while confronting them with their own image, you speak to them, but you hold a mirror in front of your chest so they're in a self-reflective face-off, or some such thing . . . I sense that she is shaken by my explanations, a new world is opening up in her head . . . she makes Azor and Mira stay on the pavement, but nothing happens, their turgid, saffron-fuzzed anuses stubbornly remain dry! —will you look at that! they're completely out of whack, to think that normally, a mere glimpse of the gutter —what was that exercise you were doing, earlier? —it's so they don't make a mess on the sidewalk, of course. Look at those stinkers, they know we're talking about them! . . . the two canines are squirming with delight —yes, but what I was saying is true, good day, Madame Chinon . . . and I went inside, where two art projects in urgent need of finishing awaited me on my desk, but I still took a moment to locate a very serious magazine called *TeckniArt*, which a colleague left at my place, containing a feature story entitled "USA: Psychotherapy at Every Stage." The guy who wrote it is a true believer, he starts with work being done with nearly naked women who are seven to nine months pregnant (there are photos) and who talk to their bellies to give their fetuses a head start in learning their mother tongue, the practice is called "systematic prenatal intelligence," just picture it, a dozen women standing in a big room in a residential Washington neighborhood not far from the White House . . . they're shouting "light! light! light!" and each time they turn on a powerful flashlight and point it at their bellies, so that the fetuses thus addressed will grasp the meaning of the word "light" and associate it with fleshly in utero illumination, and who knows, perhaps even apprehend the radiance of the Holy Ghost and the Immaculate Conception before poking their heads out into the world . . . alternatively, the women shout "music! music! music!" while blasting Carl Orff's *Carmina Burana* at their bellies, which become drum heads and acoustic membranes for the occasion, it's amazing, the reporter claims this produces early readers and music lovers; then it's on to domesticated animals, especially dogs, horses are harder to come by, cats are standoffish, and results are difficult to measure with turtles/hamsters/boa constrictors/rabbits/etcetera, but dogs are ideal subjects, exposed as they are to the full flood of their owners' neuroses . . . hence the need for efforts to bring this little world together. Now picture an identical room, occupied this time by another dozen people sitting cross-legged with large mirrors propped on their thighs, dogs sitting on the carpet opposite them, . . . the owners loudly and clearly chant slogans like: "you are not my slave!" "free yourself!" "let's accept our relationship!" and "you are your own being!" and now you'll have some of the dogs looking in the mirror, others gnawing at their fleas or licking their asses, some howling, and one is licking his mistress's radiant face . . . truly amazing, and they say the animals suffer far fewer cysts, cancers, morbid depressions, and anorexia, ticks no longer dare jump into their fur, and the dogs and their owners accept and work on their emotions, again according to the specialized *TeckniArt* reporter, who lists three essential books in his bibliography: *My Dogs and I*, by Kevina Bush, the President's eldest daughter; *Psychopathology of My Dog's Life*, by Pamela Rose; and *Buddhism and Animal Therapy*, by Liang Tsu Forster. Marie-Laure has her work cut out for her! . . . I'm eating my breakfast when I see her set off for her bridge game, impeccable as ever in an aubergine-colored suit and a black hat with a veil, so out comes the ground meat from the fridge rolled into fresh balls in which I'm increasing the dose of magnesium chloride on a daily basis, we don't want Azor and Mira's guts to get habituated to it . . . they're now living on the lawn permanently, Marie-Laure doesn't dare bring them inside while they're suffering from their "irrational incontinence". . . they rush over to the fence, barking, their tails aquiver, eager for their favorite food . . . they know their dietitian well, and wolf down their kilo of pure meat without complaint . . .

The next morning, Friday, was the turning point . . . Julia and Yasmé were at school, I park not far from the house and spot Marie-Laure ten yards ahead of me, primped and chic in gray linen pants, a green flowered jacket, and a white blouse, holding her doggies by their leather leash and carrying a basket in her other hand, off to do her shopping . . . but Azor and Mira's deportment isn't as smooth as usual, they seem preoccupied by their hindquarters: back legs stiff and slightly spread apart, tails rigid as flagpoles held up by an invisible guy line, painful, camellia-red anuses exposed to the slightest cooling breeze; the pair are obviously under severe siege from the rear . . . and suddenly, like some furrow-marking machine, they begin squirting caramel-colored humors onto the glistening pavement in two irregular parallel lines, without either rushing to the gutter or freezing in place, no, no, they simply continue on their walk as if they'd forgotten all about sphincter control and anal reflexes, breathing, walking, and shitting in a single amorphous continuum . . . Marie-Laure screams: Azor! Mira! how could you? She is yanking hysterically on the leash, dragged along a trail of liquid shit, hopping from one foot to another for fear of soiling her white canvas shoes . . . at last the pair come to halt, heads hung, directing a baleful, bitter gaze at their mistress, whose glance sweeps the street, gauging the extent of the mess . . . and yes, there I am, twenty yards away, I SAW YOU! —ah, Monsieur Marconi, I'm at my wits' end . . . I approached her, sympathetic . . . this is going to be a big cleanup job, for sure, your dogs are a bit old, aren't they? they're getting incontinent —what do you mean? they aren't even four yet! barely in their prime —prime, well, I'm not so sure about that, the power of the internal organs can't be overestimated, you know, and consider the perfect harmony between their twin sphincters, Madame Chinon . . . good luck, I mean it, good luck! . . . and I pretend to walk away —did you . . . did you find that article? —oh, yes, I have it for you, it seems the psychotherapeutic approach is impressive, the results are quite remarkable, but if you go for group therapy, shouldn't you put diapers on them while you wait for the treatment to take effect, after all this, ah, fecal pollution, in this neighborhood, it's rather shocking, don't you think, shit on the sidewalks, now that's France for you, and our children . . . —come, come, Monsieur Marconi, let's not exaggerate . . . a quick hose-down —yes, while it's still fresh . . . anyway do come by whenever you like for the magazine, but come without your mountainous defecators —my what? —your dogs . . .

Once back home, I watched her from my office . . . she had changed into a blue nylon windbreaker and rubber boots, and was cleaning the sidewalk with hose and broom, that's good, she's keeping busy, didn't dare ask her housekeeper, Eugenia, who was there this morning. An hour later, she rings the doorbell: bright yellow suit, pale gold blouse, high heels, my throat tightens . . . come in! . . . yes, yes, it's the first time, she is already appraising everything, furniture, carpets, good and bad taste, price at auction . . . it irritates me —here you are, Madame Chinon, take a look at the article, "USA: Psychotherapy at Every Stage," it's mind-boggling, I say, are you wearing Jicky, by any chance? —what a man! why yes, it's been my perfume for the last fifteen years . . . a first smile . . . —sit down, please! can I get you some coffee? —no thanks, but I'd like tea —perfect, I'll make you some, make yourself comfortable . . . I disappear into the kitchen, leaving her to her prying, come back with the tray, cups-teapot-cookies, find her absorbed in her reading . . . —very impressive, this confrontation between the animal and human kingdoms, with communication between them flowing as freely as the air we breathe, we used to do this sort of thing with our executives, but this is sensational, and here in France, we're so inclined to medicalize everything, we're not open to this kind of research, we're too logical, don't you think? it's always Descartes, Descartes, Descartes . . . her gaze falters, she catches herself . . . for example, my vet prescribes pills to make them constipated, "to reverse the process," as he says, but they aren't eating a thing! how can I give them the pills? And besides, that's not addressing the cause! it didn't even occur to him that it might be a double psychosis, not for a sin-gle-sec-ond!!! I feel sure this therapy here would work wonders with Azor and Mira, I know them very well, after all! and look here, they refer to three books that go into it further, okay, I'm getting these today, thank you so very much, Monsieur Marconi, and don't worry, we'll get through this . . . —I feel quite sure of it Madame . . . —listen, we're neighbors, won't you call me Marie-Laure? . . . —why, with pleasure, Madame Chinon! . . . and there we were, sharing a laugh . . . Just joking, Marie-Laure, and please call me Ettore, my dear neighbor, or Hector, if you prefer, and besides it rhymes: Marie-Laure/Hector . . . —ah, how charming he is . . . I begin to feel a tingling in my testicles near the base of my penis, here is my dream neighbor sitting there with her sheath skirt hiked halfway up her thigh, ah, Marie-Laure! . . . —by the way, will you think about my suggestion in the meantime? about the diapers, I mean, I feel sure it will take some of the pressure off you.

Translated by William Rodarmor

The Womanizer

Frédéric Fajardie

THE NIGHTCLUB was illuminated like an aquarium in a Chinese restaurant, with a few pathetic lasers flashing through the air.

As our man stepped inside he put on a look of resigned weariness, the look of a great predator who'd wandered off the savannah and into a rabbit hutch somewhere out by Saint-Chéron.

An attitude he figured would intrigue the many women who were present.

Except that no one paid any attention to him.

It was a quiet Saturday night in Romainville, the kind of night our hero looked forward to. He was an all-terrain pickup artist who'd burned his bridges in the Paris dating scene and was now exploring the suburbs.

FRÉDÉRIC FAJARDIE (1947–2008) was one of France's most prolific short-story writers. His *Nouvelles d'un siècle l'autre* (2000) includes 365 stories he wrote from the 1970s to the turn of the millennium. He was also a novelist, screenwriter, and detective-story author. Fajardie's books include *La nuit des chats bottés* (1979), *Les foulards rouges* (2001), and *Le voleur de vent* (2003). This story is from his 1990 collection, *Chrysalide des villes*.

He'd reasoned that Romainville would be a good hunting ground, with its housing projects and neighborhoods of little bungalows with yards that look sad—except maybe to their owners, who struggled to grow geraniums or, given the tough economic times, leeks.

All that social mixing should logically produce a greater variety of prey and thereby increase his chances of success.

He'd scouted the burb and quickly located the site of his future exploits: the Nuits de Chine, an old bar remodeled as a nightclub, which offered karaoke on Saturday nights.

Our loser—he was what the French call a *blaireau*—was over fifty, with nice brown hair that had largely surrendered to an aggressive assault of baldness, gleaming false teeth, and impressive abs, which he cleverly hid under layers of fat so as not to seem ostentatious. Let's be honest: our hunter wasn't exactly in his prime.

He was wearing a navy blazer he'd bought in London eight years earlier and whose buttons he could no longer fasten, a blindingly white shirt hungry for soup stains, one of his father's club ties from the thirties, and gray slacks. To add a youthful note, he wore American Sebago loafers.

When he signed up for the karaoke, he realized it might be a bust from the start, because the only songs left to choose from were "Dactylos Rock" and Françoise Hardy's old hit, "Tous les garçons et les filles."

For the next two dreary hours, he kept asking himself, "What the hell am I doing here, listening to all these poor assholes sing?"

The most beautiful girl in the club, who was about twenty-five, was sitting in the front row. He could see her only in three-quarter profile.

The ideal prey. He was nobody's fool. A young woman might prefer to go out with guys her own age, but . . .

He studied her: sweet, fresh, very pretty—and of course lacking in experience. An area where our hunter considered himself a real expert, as it happens. Besides, life had proved him right, ever since he'd found the ideal demographic: a woman between twenty-five and thirty, newly married and already disappointed by her young husband's inexperience. These were young women who felt the need to be introduced to real lovemaking. If they hesitated, he would deliver an irrefutable argument.

"Your husband will be the main beneficiary, since he'll be able to enjoy it every day. It isn't cheating, it's an act of kindness!"

As dismaying as it may seem, the fact is, it worked!

It was his turn.

He set down his fourth scotch with a gesture that bespoke a man with real class and climbed onto the pathetic little stage of the Nuits de Chine in Romainville, Seine-Saint-Denis. He felt a little nervous, just the same: it was his first karaoke.

Music filled the room, lyrics scrolled down the screen, and he began to sing. He immediately grasped the iron rule of karaoke: nobody listens to anybody. He'd been bored listening to the others, and now it was his turn to bore them.

But a real playboy doesn't give up in the face of adversity. In spite of the very curvaceous young prey in the front row, who was loudly comparing the respective merits of René Dhéry and Naf-Naf clothes with her girlfriend, in spite of the crummy audience, which was paying him no more attention than if he'd been a pressure cooker parked on the stage and jiggling his little top, he bravely began to sing.

"All the boys and girls my age walk the streets two by two . . ."

How long had it been since he last sang that old song?

"All the boys and girls my age know what it means to be two . . ."

The first time he'd heard it must have been 1962. Or was it?

"Looking into each other's eyes, holding hands, they're in love and unafraid of tomorrow . . ."

Yes, it was 1962. He already liked girls by then, but not at all in the way he did now. He still remembered the first time he heard that song. He was on vacation in the Vosges. Ah, the laughs, the blueberry bushes, the walks along the streams with friends, boys and girls, the old transistor radio!

"But I walk the streets alone, my soul in pain. I'm alone, because nobody loves me . . ."

Papa and Maman, now dead, had met him at the Gare de l'Est and almost didn't recognize him, he'd grown so much. How old was he then? Fourteen, nearly fifteen.

He softly repeated, "Nobody loves me . . ."

He felt like crying, and against his will, two big tears ran down his cheeks.

It was true. Our poor old blaireau didn't have a papa or a maman anymore, his wife had divorced him, and his children thought he was a loser.

Unable to go on singing, he watched the lyrics scrolling

by as if they were a personal message sent by some obscure power whose job it was to make him feel bad.

"My days and my nights are exactly alike, joyless but anxious, with nobody to whisper, 'I love you' in my ear . . ."

The audience, glad to rouse itself from its growing torpor and liven up the mood—thanks, *Saturday Night Fever*—began to hoot.

With great dignity, he set the mic down and returned to his scotch.

The blaireau couldn't remember exactly how many scotches he'd drunk. Eight or nine, maybe more.

He also didn't know who the woman was sitting opposite him at his table, or why he was talking to her.

"My idea was to make love to all the women I met. That's something my ex could never accept."

She was a rather attractive forty-year-old. She observed him for a moment, then asked, "Why all of them?"

He gestured helplessly.

"No idea. In any case, that's the way it is. I can't help it. It's not my fault. I've got an affective pathology that goes back to childhood, since I was a little boy, anyway. Emotional deprivation, my mother didn't really love me, and that's probably what drives me to compulsively repeat a sexual act I don't expect much from, except maybe the hope of wearying myself, given the many women who fall into my arms."

"Well put!" she remarked.

Emboldened, he went on. "Yes, but it's more complicated than that. You've got to factor in a desire for social revenge. If I make love to a judge's daughter, it's like I'm fucking the whole judiciary, see?"

She brought the conversation around. "What about older women? After all, there's more than just chicks out there."

He thought for a moment, then lowered his voice.

"Older women are like desirable whores I want to punish for . . . I don't know, maybe just for being desirable."

"And the only punishment is getting your rocks off?"

"Afraid so."

They exchanged a first smile. "What kind of work do you do?" she asked.

"I'm an economist. I work at the Centre national de la recherche scientifique. What about you?"

"I teach Spanish."

He seemed surprised.

"Er . . . So what're you doing here in Romainville on a Saturday night?"

"Same as you, I assume: as far as the Paris pickup scene goes, I'm totally burned."

She stood up, took her purse, and gestured for him to follow her.

"They say I'm a bit of a nympho, but that's because they can't satisfy me. With me, you won't have time to go looking anywhere else or indulging in fantasies."

"But what about my past? I'm a womanizer, a creep."

"Yeah, that's pretty much what I figured."

He followed her, very excited at the idea of being treated like a sex object.

Translated by William Rodarmor

Two Bodies on a Barge

Georges Simenon

THE LOCKKEEPER of Le Coudray was a lean, depressed-looking fellow in a corduroy suit, with drooping mustaches and a suspicious eye, like a typical estate bailiff. He made no distinction between Maigret and the fifty other people—gendarmes, journalists, policemen from Corbeil and representatives of the Department of Public Prosecution—to whom he had told his story over the past two days. And as he spoke he kept a watchful eye, upstream and downstream, over the gray-green surface of the Seine.

It was November. The weather was cold and a bleak pale sky was reflected in the water.

GEORGES SIMENON (1903–1989) was one of the hardest-working writers in history. His oeuvre includes nearly 200 novels, more than 150 novellas, several autobiographical works, numerous articles, and scores of pulp novels written under more than two dozen pseudonyms. But Simenon is best known for his 75 novels and 28 short stories featuring Inspector Maigret, the pipe-smoking Paris police detective. The first novel in the series, *Pietr-le-Letton*, appeared in 1931; the last one, *Maigret et M. Charles*, was published in 1972. This story appears in Simenon's 1977 collection, *Maigret's Pipe*.

"I had to get up at six this morning to look after my wife." (Maigret reflected that these decent, sad-eyed men are always the ones who have sick wives to look after.) "While I was lighting the fire I thought I heard something. But it was only later, while I was up on the first floor preparing her poultice, that I realized somebody was calling. I came downstairs. I went out on to the lock, and there I could vaguely make out a dark mass against the weir . . .

"'What's up?' I shouted.

"'Help!' somebody called out hoarsely.

"'What are you doing there?' I asked.

"And he went on shouting: 'Help!'

"I took my wherry to go after him. I could see it was the *Astrolabe*. As it was beginning to get light at last, I made out old Claessens on deck. I could take my oath that he was still tight and that he had no idea what his barge was doing up against the lock. The dog was loose, and indeed I asked him to hold on to it. And that's it."

The important thing, from his point of view, was that a barge had run into his lock and might have damaged it if the current had been stronger. He seemed totally unconcerned by the fact that, apart from the drunken old carter and a big Alsatian dog, there had been nobody on board but two corpses, a man and a woman, both hanged.

The *Astrolabe* had been released and was now moored a hundred and fifty meters away, guarded by a constable who kept himself warm pacing up and down the towpath. It was an old barge without a motor, a "stable-boat," as they call those barges that travel along canals with their horses on board. Passing cyclists turned to stare at this grayish hull, about which all the papers had been talking for the past two days.

As usual, when Superintendent Maigret had been brought in, it was because there were no fresh clues to be noted. Everybody had gone into the case, and the witnesses had already been questioned fifty times, first by the local gendarmerie, then by the Corbeil police, by magistrates, and by reporters.

"You'll see, it was Emile Gradut who committed the crime," he had been told.

And Maigret, after spending two hours questioning Gradut, was back on the scene of the incident, his hands in the pockets of his heavy overcoat, looking cross and staring at the gloomy landscape as though he was considering buying a plot of land there.

The interest lay not in the lock at Coudray into which the barge had crashed, but at the other end of the reach, eight kilometers higher upstream at the lock of La Citanguette.

The setting here was much the same as lower down. The villages of Morsang and Seine-Port were on the opposite bank, a longish way off, so that there was nothing to be seen but the quiet water with copses beside it and the occasional scar of an old gravel pit.

But at La Citanguette there was a bistro, and boats did their utmost to spend the night there. It was a real boatmen's bistro where they sold bread, canned goods, sausage, tackle, and oats for the horses.

And that was really where Maigret conducted his inquiry, without appearing to do so, taking a drink from time to time, sitting down by the stove or taking a turn outside while the *patronne*, who was so fair as to be almost an albino, watched him with slightly ironical respect.

About that Wednesday evening the following facts were known. When it was beginning to get dark, the *Aiglon VII*, a small tug from the upper Seine, had brought its six lighters, like a brood of ducklings, up to the Citanguette lock. It was drizzling at the time. When the boats were moored the men forgathered as usual in the bistro for a drink, while the lockkeeper took in his cranks.

The *Astrolabe* came round the river bend only half an hour later, by which time darkness had fallen. Old Arthur Aerts, the skipper, was at the wheel, while Claessens walked along the towpath in front of his horses with his whip over his shoulder.

Then the *Astrolabe* had moored behind the string of boats, and Claessens had taken his horses on board. At that point nobody had paid attention to them.

It was seven o'clock at least and everyone had finished eating when Aerts and Claessens came into the bistro and sat down by the stove. The skipper of the *Aiglon VII* was doing most of the talking, and the two old men did not speak. The white-haired *patronne*, with a baby in her arms, served them four or five glasses of marc, but she had taken little notice of them.

That was how it had been, Maigret now realized. All these people were more or less acquainted with one another. They would come in with a brief gesture of greeting and sit down without a word. Sometimes a woman would come in, just to buy provisions for the next day and then to warn her husband, as he sat there drinking: "Don't be back too late."

That had been the case with Aerts's wife Emma, who had bought bread, eggs, and a rabbit.

From that point onward every detail acquired crucial importance, every piece of evidence became extremely valuable. And so Maigret persisted.

"You're sure that when he left about ten o'clock Arthur Aerts was drunk?"

"Quite tight, as usual," the proprietress replied. "He was a Belgian, a good fellow on the whole, who always sat in his corner saying nothing and went on drinking till he'd just got strength enough left to go back to his boat."

"And Claessens the carter?"

"He could take a bit more. He stayed about a quarter of an hour longer, then he went off, after coming back for his whip, which he'd forgotten."

So far, so good. It was easy to picture the banks of the Seine at night, below the lock, the tug with its six lighters behind it, then Aerts's barge, with a lamp hanging over each boat and the steady drizzle pouring down over it all.

About half past nine Emma had gone back on board the barge with her provisions. At ten, Aerts had gone back himself, quite tight, as the *patronne* had said. And at a quarter past the carter had at last made his way back to the *Astrolabe*.

"I was only waiting for him to leave to close down, because boatmen go to bed early and there was nobody else left."

So much was reliable evidence and could be confirmed; but it was all. After that, not the smallest piece of exact information. At six in the morning the skipper of the tug had been surprised not to see the *Astrolabe* behind his lighters, and a little later he had noticed that the moorings had been cut.

At the same moment the lockkeeper at Le Coudray, who was looking after his sick wife, had heard the shouts of the old carter, and soon afterwards had discovered that the barge had run into his weir.

The dog was running loose on the deck. The carter, woken up by the collision, knew nothing and declared that he had been asleep all night in his stable as usual.

Only, in the cabin at the back of the boat, Aerts's body was discovered; he had been hanged, not with a rope but with the dog's chain. Then, behind a curtain that concealed the washbasin, his wife Emma was found hanging too; she had been hanged with a sheet taken from the bed.

And that was not all, since just before setting forth, the skipper of the *Aiglon VII*, after vainly calling for his stoker Emile Gradut, discovered that the man had disappeared.

"Gradut was the murderer . . ."

Everybody was convinced of it, and that very evening the newspapers were full of such headlines as: "Gradut seen prowling around Seine-Port," "Manhunt in Rougeau Forest," "Aerts's hoard still not found."

For all evidence went to prove that old Aerts had had a hoard, and indeed everyone agreed on the sum: a hundred thousand francs. It was a long yet quite simple story. Aerts, who was sixty and had two grown-up, married sons, had married as his second wife Emma, a tough Strasbourgeoise twenty years his junior.

Things were not going at all well between the couple. At every lock they stopped at, Emma would grumble about the miserliness of the old man, who scarcely gave her enough to eat.

"I don't even know where he keeps his money," she would say. "He wants his sons to have it when he dies. And meanwhile I have to kill myself looking after him and steering the boat; not to mention . . ."

She would add crude details, sometimes in front of Aerts himself, while he just shook his head stubbornly. Then, after she had left, he would mutter:

"She only married me for my hundred thousand francs, but she's going to be disappointed."

Emma would comment, furthermore:

"As though his sons needed it to live on!"

In fact the elder son, Joseph, was the skipper of a tug-boat at Antwerp, while Theodore, with his father's help, had bought a fine self-propelled barge, the *Marie-France*. He had been notified of his father's death while passing through Maestricht, in Holland.

"But I'm going to find those hundred thousand francs of his."

She would tell you all this out of the blue, when she'd only known you five minutes, giving the most intimate details about her old husband, and adding cynically:

"He surely can't suppose that it was out of love that a young woman like myself . . ."

And she was unfaithful to him. The evidence was indisputable. Even the skipper of the *Aiglon VII* knew about it.

"I can only tell you what I know. But it's a fact that

during the fortnight we were lying idle at Alfortville and the *Astrolabe* was being loaded, Emile Gradut often went to meet her, even in broad daylight."

So what next?

Emile Gradut, twenty-three years of age, was a bad character, that was obvious. He had, in fact, been caught after twenty-four hours, half starved, in the Rougeau Forest, less than five kilometers from La Citanguette.

"I've done nothing!" he yelled at the policemen, as he tried to ward off their blows.

A nasty little ruffian with whom Maigret had been closeted for two hours in his office and who kept stubbornly repeating:

"I've done nothing."

"Then why did you run away?"

"That's my business!"

As for the examining magistrate, convinced that Gradut had hidden the hoard in the forest, he had fresh searches made there in vain.

There was something infinitely dreary about it all, as dreary as the river, which reflected the same sky from morning till night, or those strings of boats that announced their arrival with a blast from a hooter (one blast for each barge being towed) as they threaded their way into the lock in an endless stream. Then, while the women stayed on deck to look after the children and keep an eye on the movements of the boat, the men went up to the bistro for a drink and then walked slowly back.

"It's plain sailing," one of his colleagues had said to Maigret.

And yet Maigret, as sullen as the Seine itself, as sullen as a canal in the rain, had returned to his lock and could not bring himself to leave it.

It's always the same story: when a case seems too clear-cut, nobody bothers to probe it in detail. Everybody agreed that Gradut was the criminal, and he had such a villainous look about him that it seemed self-evident.

Nonetheless, the results of the post mortem had now come in and they led to some curious conclusions. Thus in the case of Arthur Aerts, Dr. Paul said:

"Slight bruising at the base of the chin . . . From the state of rigor mortis and the contents of the stomach it can be specified that death by strangulation occurred between 10 and 10:30 PM."

Now Aerts had gone back on board at ten o'clock. According to the white-haired *patronne*, Claessens had followed him a quarter of an hour later, and Claessens declared that he had gone straight into his cabin.

"Was there a light in the Aerts's cabin?"

"I don't know."

"Was the dog tied up?"

The poor old fellow had thought for a long time, but had finally made a helpless gesture. No, he didn't know. He hadn't noticed. How could he have foretold that it would matter so much what he did that particular evening? He had been drowsy with drink as usual; he slept in his clothes, on the straw, lying cozily beside his horse and his mare.

"You heard no noise?"

He didn't know! He couldn't have known! He had gone to sleep, and when he woke up he had found himself in midstream, up against the weir.

At this point, however, there was a piece of evidence. But could it be taken seriously? It came from Madame Couturier, the wife of the skipper of the *Aiglon VII*. The head of the Corbeil police had questioned her like everyone else before letting the train of boats carry on its journey towards the Loing Canal. Maigret had the report in his pocket.

Q. Did you hear anything during the night?

A. I wouldn't swear to it.

Q. Tell us what you heard.

A. It's so uncertain. I woke up at one point and looked at the time on my alarm clock. It was a quarter to eleven. I thought I heard people speaking near the boat.

Q. Did you recognize the voices?

A. No. But I thought it must be Gradut meeting Emma. I must have fallen asleep immediately after . . .

Could one rely on this? And even if it was true, what did it prove?

Below the lock, the tugboat and its six lighters and the *Astrolabe* had been lying quiet that night and . . .

As regards Aerts, the report was definite: he had died of strangulation between 10:00 and 10:30 PM.

But things became more complicated when it came to the second report, the one about Emma.

"The left cheek shows contusions produced either by a blunt instrument or by a violent blow with someone's fist . . . Death, due to asphyxia by hanging, must have taken place at about 1:00 AM."

And Maigret became ever more deeply absorbed in the slow, ponderous life of La Citanguette, as though only there was he capable of thought. A self-propelled barge flying a Belgian flag reminded him of Theodore, Aerts's son, who must by now have reached Paris.

At the same time, the Belgian flag suggested the thought of gin. For on the table in the cabin there had been found a bottle of gin, more than half empty. Somebody had made a thorough search of the cabin itself and even torn open the mattress covers, scattering the flock stuffing.

Obviously, in an attempt to find the hidden hoard of a hundred thousand francs!

The first investigators had declared: "It's quite simple! Emile Gradut killed Aerts and Emma. Then he got drunk and hunted for the treasure, which he hid in the forest." Only. Yes! Only Dr. Paul, in his post-mortem on Emma's body, had found in her stomach all the gin that was missing from the bottle!

Clearly, since Emma had drunk the gin, it couldn't have been Gradut!

"Sure!" the investigators had replied. "Gradut, after killing Aerts, had made the woman tipsy in order to overcome her more easily, for she was a strong creature, don't forget."

So that if they were right, Gradut and his mistress must have stayed on board from 10:00 or 10:30 PM, the time of Aerts's death, until midnight or 1:00 AM, the time of Emma's.

It was possible, of course. Everything was possible. Only Maigret wanted, somehow or other, to get to understand the bargees' way of thinking.

He had been as harsh as the rest with Emile Gradut. For two hours he had grilled him thoroughly. To begin with he had tried the wheedling method, *la chansonnette,* as they said at the Quai des Orfèvres.

"Listen, old man. You're involved, that's clear. But to be frank with you, I don't believe you killed the pair of them."

"I've done nothing!"

"You didn't kill them, that's for sure. But admit that you knocked the old fellow about a bit. It was his own fault, of course. He caught you together, and so in self-defense . . ."

"I've done nothing!"

"As for Emma, of course you didn't touch her, since she was your woman."

"You're wasting your time! I've done nothing."

Afterwards Maigret had become harsher, even threatening.

"Oh, so that's how it is. Well, we shall see, once you're on that boat with the two bodies."

But Gradut hadn't even flinched at the prospect of a reconstruction of the crime.

"Whenever you like. I've done nothing."

"All the same, when we find the money you've put away somewhere . . ."

Then Emile Gradut gave a smile. A smile of pity. An infinitely superior smile.

That evening the only vessels moored at La Citanguette were one motorized barge and a stable-boat. By the lower lock, a policeman was still on duty on the deck of the *Astrolabe,* and he was greatly surprised when Maigret, climbing up on board, announced:

"I haven't time to go back to Paris. I'll sleep here."

The soft lapping of water could be heard against the hull, and the footsteps of the policeman as he paced the deck for fear of going to sleep. The poor man began to wonder whether Maigret wasn't going out of his mind. All alone inside the boat, he was making as much noise as if the two horses had been let loose in the hold.

"Excuse me, officer," Maigret emerged from the hatchway. "Could you possibly get hold of a pickaxe for me?"

Get hold of a pickaxe at ten o'clock at night, in such a spot? However, the policeman woke up the sad-looking lockkeeper, who, being a gardener, owned a pickaxe.

"What does your Super want to do with it?"

"Damned if I know!"

And they exchanged significant glances. As for Maigret, he went back into the cabin with his pickaxe, and for an hour after that the policeman heard muffled blows.

"Look here, officer . . ."

It was Maigret again, sweating and out of breath, thrusting his head through the hatchway.

"Go and put through a phone call for me. I'd like the examining magistrate to come as early as possible tomorrow morning and have Emile Gradut brought along."

The lockkeeper had never looked so lugubrious as when he guided the examining magistrate to the barge, while Gradut followed, flanked by a couple of policemen.

"No. I swear I don't know anything!"

Maigret was asleep on the Aerts's bed. He didn't even apologize, and seemed unaware of the magistrate's stupefaction at the sight of the cabin.

The floorboards had been lifted. Underneath there was a layer of cement, but this had been smashed with the pickaxe, and the mess was indescribable.

"Come in, Monsieur le juge. I was very late getting to bed and I haven't had time to tidy myself up yet."

He lit a pipe. He had found some bottles of beer somewhere and he poured himself a drink.

"Come in, Gradut. And now . . ."

"Yes, now?" asked the magistrate.

"It's quite simple," Maigret declared, puffing at his pipe. "I'll explain what happened the other night. You see, there was one thing that struck me from the first: old Aerts had been hanged *with a chain* and his wife *with a sheet*.

"You'll soon understand. Study police records and I'll swear you'll never find a single case of a man hanging himself with a wire or a chain. It may be odd, but it's so. Suicides are sensitive people and the thought of those links bruising their throats and pinching the skin of their necks . . ."

"So Arthur Aerts was murdered?"

"That's my conclusion, yes, particularly since the bruise that was noticed on his chin seems to prove that the chain, having been slipped round his neck from behind while he was drunk, struck his face first."

"I don't see . . ."

"Wait a minute! Now note that his wife, on the other hand, had been hanged with a twisted sheet. Not even a rope, whereas there are plenty of them on board a boat. No, a sheet off a bed, which is the gentlest way of hanging oneself, so to speak."

"And that means?"

"That she hanged herself. She even had to swallow half a liter of gin to get up her courage, whereas normally she never drank. Remember the forensic report."

"I remember it."

"So we have one murder and one suicide, the murder committed at about a quarter past ten, the suicide at midnight or 1:00 AM. And that makes everything as clear as daylight."

The magistrate was watching him somewhat suspiciously, and Emile Gradut with ironic curiosity.

"For a long time now," Maigret went on, "Emma, who had not got what she hoped for from her marriage to old Aerts and who was in love with Emile Gradut, had been obsessed by one idea: to get hold of the hoard and run away with her lover. Suddenly an opportunity arose. Aerts came home dead drunk. Gradut was close by, on board the tug. She'd already noticed, when she went to buy her provisions in the bistro, that her husband was pretty tipsy. So she unfastened the dog and waited, with the chain all ready to be slipped round the man's neck."

"But . . ." the magistrate objected.

"Presently! Let me finish. Now, Aerts is dead. Emma, elated with her triumph, runs to fetch Gradut; don't forget, at this point, that the wife of the tugboat skipper had heard voices close to her boat at a quarter to eleven. Isn't that true, Gradut?"

"It's true."

"The couple comes on board to look for the treasure, searches everywhere, even inside the mattress, but fails to find those hundred thousand francs. Is that true, Gradut?"

"It's true."

"Time passes and Gradut grows impatient. He even wonders, I'd be willing to bet, if he's not been had, if those hundred thousand francs really exist. Emma swears they do. But what use are they if they can't be found? So they keep on searching. Then Gradut gets fed up. He knows he'll be accused of the crime. He wants to clear off. Emma wants to go with him."

"Excuse me . . ." the magistrate tried to put in.

"Presently! I tell you she wants to go off with him and, since he has no desire to be burdened with a woman who hasn't even any money, he solves the problem by knocking her out with his fist. Having floored her, he cuts the moorings of the barge. Is that true, Gradut?"

This time Gradut seemed reluctant to reply.

"That's about all," Maigret concluded. "If they had discovered the treasure they'd have gone off together, or else they'd have tried to make the old man's death look like suicide. Since they've failed to find it, Gradut takes fright, and roams through the countryside trying to take cover. Emma, when she comes round, finds the boat drifting downstream and the hanged man swinging by her side. No hope left for her, not even the hope of escape. It would mean waking Claessens to guide the barge with the boathook. In short, the whole thing has been a fiasco. And she decides to kill herself. Only her courage fails her, so she drinks first and then takes a soft sheet from the bed."

"Is this true, Gradut?" asked the magistrate, watching the young thug.

"Since the Super says so . . ."

"But wait a minute," the magistrate objected. "What is

to prove that he didn't find the treasure and, in order to keep it . . ."

Then Maigret merely kicked aside some pieces of cement and disclosed a hiding place with Belgian and French gold coins.

"Do you understand now?"

"More or less," the magistrate muttered, without much conviction.

And Maigret, filling a fresh pipe, growled:

"One had to know, in the first place, that they use a cement foundation for repairing old barges. Nobody told me that."

Then, with a sudden change of tone:

"The oddest thing about it is that I've counted, and there really are a hundred thousand francs. A peculiar household, don't you think?"

Translated by Jean Stewart

Rue Laferrière

Jacques Réda

MAPS THAT SHOW IT bending like an elbow or even, approximately, describing a quarter of a circle, don't begin to convey the feeling you get when you turn into rue Laferrière unexpectedly. This is down at the very end of rue Henri-Monnier, which ends there in a most peculiar way. More often than not, streets complete their course as if their deepest wish was to continue it, assuming nothing prevents them from doing so. But generally speaking they encounter two main kinds of obstacle: brutal interruption by a cross street, or—far more disconcertingly since it's only theoretical—a simple change of name, sometimes more or less warranted by a slight adjustment of angle or curve. In both cases, it seems as if despite their reservations

---

JACQUES RÉDA (1929–) is a poet, jazz critic, and flâneur who was the chief editor of the *Nouvelle Revue Française* from 1987 to 1996. His books include *Récitatif* (1970, tr. *The Party is Over*), *Les ruines de Paris* (1977, tr. *Ruins of Paris*), and *Retour au calme* (1989, tr. *Return to Calm*). "Rue Laferrière" is from his 2001 collection, *Accidents de la circulation*. Neil Blackadder's translation appeared in *Two Lines*, the magazine of the Center for the Art of Translation, in San Francisco, in 2007.

and the momentum they've built up, streets submit to this frustrating situation without questioning it—that they say to themselves, "Let's not talk about it," and through their awareness of their own personality, they regain what all of a sudden has been denied by space to their ambitions, their dreams, and their desires. Would they like to become avenues? They know that if they did they would lose some of their character and some of their meaning, and this helps them to agree willingly to the limits imposed upon them. After all, avenues, for the most part (if we set aside exceptions like Soeur-Rosalie, in the thirteenth, whose width almost has the upper hand over its length), are not fundamentally interested in themselves. Oriented toward the outside world, which calls to them and which they have at least the illusion of conquering and organizing, they have no appreciable inner life, no taste for introspection. They like pomp, glory, and the expansive motion that launches them straight into open spaces and thereby magnifies their splendor. Streets are egocentric, attentive, sometimes to the point of hypochondria, to their feelings of discomfort, and to their flaws, or on the contrary almost too pleased with incidental oddities that they show off to a rather ridiculous extent. While avenues attempt, sometimes with success, to join the chorus of grand impersonal categories such as space, time, order, and beauty, streets remain individuals of a complex and contradictory nature and one has to accept them as they are, or risk never managing to discern those positive qualities that are rarely separable from their failings.

And given that state of affairs, here is what makes rue Henri-Monnier stand out: it doesn't simply agree to come to an end, as the vast majority of streets do. Beveled off as it is by rue Notre-Dame-de-Lorette, it completely transforms this ending to its own advantage. It is as if all at once rue Henri-Monnier decided both not to carry on and not to break off but instead to keep itself in suspense at the end of the slope where it opens out and opens up in incompleteness, thus creating a kind of square. Kind of, yes. And with the arbitrariness typical of those responsible for Parisian toponymy, this has been used as an excuse for surgically removing from rue Henri-Monnier that essential part of its being, as if it were a superfluous appendage offered up to the voracity attributed to countless applicants waiting without a word in municipal waiting rooms. That part was amputated to the benefit of Gustave Toudouze, though it is not known whether he was delighted by this honor or scandalized at being associated with the misdeed. The business is relatively recent, since a street map I own from 1925 makes no mention of it. It's true that the same thing happened to the creator of Joseph Prudhomme. He was forced upon one Bréda who, in 1830, had seen off a different namesake. Besides, when they're not actually indicating in an explicit way where their mission takes them (rue du Puits, rue de la Gare, rue de l'Église, rue du Pré), street names are of negligible importance. All the more so since often the meadow, the well, and even the station have long since disappeared. In such cases the name's persistence takes an ironic or sarcastic turn that can harm the street. So it makes more sense to forget the names of streets, if you want to become acquainted with them intimately and authentically. Among all the spaces designated for urban peregrination, there is one we call

Henri-Monnier, where even the least shrewd observer will notice the indisputable presence of a wholeness which incorporates (and cancels out) the purely fictitious Toudouze enclave supposedly carved out in that spot. What the onlooker will see there is, as I said, "a kind of square," but such as one finds in villages with indistinct outlines, and where actually there are neither squares nor streets because everything has contentedly abandoned itself to its instincts, like a relief map taking a siesta. The observer himself is already sinking into those dreams full of air and light that pass through our minds during afternoon naps, in summer, into which we project shadows and flashes of other times, other skies, other trees, other squares in other villages, as if the marked yet slight slope of the spot, propitious for attracting metamorphoses, at the same time kept it from drifting in the void and toward night. These places rarely occupy a geometric center, and just as seldom conceal themselves at a distance—and, when they do, they belong to a different magical design altogether, one to which we cannot lay ourselves open without peril. No. Right away we understand that the widening of rue Henri-Monnier, confiscated for Toudouze, by no means jeopardizes its equilibrium, but to the contrary situates it in a balance that is harmonious even though it feels rustic and cut off from the laws of symmetry and rationality. A triangle verging on being a rectangle, it's planted with nearly a dozen chestnut trees whose foliage can, by leaning forward, exchange secret vegetal messages with the leaves of avenue Frochot. Also to be found there: a Wallace drinking fountain, two benches, and, along the hypotenuse, as well as the Vitaneuf laundromat and the Le Roustan restaurant, two tearooms (Le Rosier de l'Inde and Tea Follies) in whose outdoor seating areas one is apparently not obliged to consume only that infusion. However, I avoid sitting down there, knowing to what degree physical immobility brings about the numbing of my mental faculties and of my sensitivity to the waves that a site can emit.

So I walk to and fro inside and around that triangle and, fatally, a few steps too many beyond rue Clauzel lead me to the entry into rue Laferrière. Which is what I wanted to talk about, but some stories need a long preamble, which is perhaps their real subject. Anyway, I set off down this street, even though it's somewhat forbidding after the village-like charm of the earlier one, but it does hold that appeal always exerted upon me (not that it makes me indifferent to views that disappear into the distance) by paths—be they in the countryside, in the forest, or man-made—whose meandering hides their trajectory from us. It is tempting for us to believe they intentionally delay the moment of a discovery that's connected, as far as its importance goes, to the number of detours it makes. Thus we end up losing our way, and that is precisely the lesson of the journey, that point of uncertainty where a really adventurous walker would know how to detect the expected revelation. But in general we force ourselves to retrace our steps. Besides, rue Laferrière doesn't offer any of those esoteric-looking complications. One does not, however, appreciate this from the outset. The resolute turn it points to could be the first in a long series. In fact it's the only one. After a hundred meters or so in a straight line, the street refracts ninety degrees, following a curve whose generous arc absorbs the brutality of the angle, to be replaced by the invitation that seems to be offered by even the smallest segment of a circle, at which point a movement begins that would at one and the same time give way to a tangential force and tend to bring us all the way back around to our point of departure. Lined with high facades, rigid and impassive, that appear to have nothing in common with the capricious and malicious undulations of a path in the woods, devoid of mystery yet nonetheless concealing the section that comes after it, the curve of rue Laferrière presents a monumental and almost harshly solemn aspect. People out walking find that a muddled world of apprehensions gets stirred up in their minds by the chance encounters of the routes they take; that world is transported by this street, which simplifies it into the realm of ideas, establishing it as a concept. Which is what gives rise to the very powerful effect rue Laferrière creates when one turns into it, between the convex bank of buildings rounded like a great tower and the concave bank which corrects their centrifugal movement. Another ten steps, and you realize you'll soon be set back down in rue Notre-Dame-de-Lorette. But there, ideally, the cycle completes itself, you're cradled in the lap of an axiom that allows you, in practical terms, to think that rue Laferrière turns again to rejoin rue Henri-Monnier, the little slanting triangle, which is where the street lends itself to all kinds of suggestions for dreams.

Translated by Neil Blackadder

Child of the Carousel
Andrée Chedid

IN A CLATTER OF WEAPONS and prayers, crusaders from France and her neighbors used to assemble in this square, which was once dominated by an impressive cathedral.

Religion and conquest went hand in hand, and these exalted, feverish warriors steeped in the rightness of their cause were preparing themselves for the eternal, ferocious tragedy: faith and carnage, conquest and terror, heroism and blood.

Today the picture is quite different, at least in this square, where just one tower of the historic church remains. It's now a peaceful little garden, where a diverse population goes about its business and leisure.

The June day was drawing deliciously to a close. Passersby of all races, ages, and appearances crossed the square on

ANDRÉE CHEDID (1920–) is a celebrated poet and novelist. Born in Cairo to Lebanese parents, she has lived in France since 1946 and has been bridging cultures ever since. In addition to some twenty-two volumes of poetry, she has written sixteen novels, seven plays, and many short stories. This story is from *Mondes Miroirs Magies* (1988). Chedid later expanded it into a novella, *L'enfant multiple* (1989, tr. *The Multiple Child*).

their way to Beaubourg, les Halles, or Châtelet. Others were strolling along the paths of this little patch of greenery, walking their dogs, or sitting on benches.

In one corner of the square, next to the Boulevard de Sébastopol, a carousel was being closed up for the night.

It was a magnificent carousel, decorated with plaster garlands and pompoms, and hung with seven oval mirrors. There were twelve roan horses with black tails, and a white horse with golden mane, bridle, and hooves. But the carousel's crown jewel was a fairy carriage with two red velvet benches that spun around to the rhythm of a popular tune of yesteryear.

Maxime Balin was proud of his carousel and its equipment. The son and grandson of civil servants, he was glad he'd barely escaped the straitjacket of bureaucracy and the rigid confines of paper pushers progressing slowly from pen to computer.

Distancing himself from his family was no hardship for Maxime; it was actually something of a relief, and they immediately started referring to him as a loser and a clown. He also enjoyed being single. At fifty, it allowed him to live his life as he pleased.

But for the last year or so, he'd been feeling depressed. As the carousel spun, he found himself reflected in each of its seven mirrors in turn. This forced him to confront his figure, which was getting heavier, and his shoulders, which were getting rounder. His black sweater could no longer hide his sagging belly. His flabby jowls and balding head were constantly reflected back to him.

Maxime was no ladies' man, though he prided himself on his many swift conquests. But attractive women had stopped looking his way for some time now; the love light was out.

In contrast, he was receiving many marks of solicitude from old ladies! Their winks and knowing remarks—which showed that they already considered him one of their own—made him shudder.

Business was slow. In the evenings, the weary carousel owner would cover his structure with an enormous waterproof canvas before setting off, earlier and earlier in the day, for his home on the outskirts of Paris.

Soon Maxime started to cut corners in small ways, though his economizing didn't do much for business. The restrictions and calculations awakened in him old habits that gave him a certain satisfaction. In skimping and saving—as a long line of his ancestors had done before him, without ever getting rich—he was reconnecting with a tradition of prudence and parsimony, which had so far eluded him.

To save on electricity, he stopped lighting the flashing bulbs. To avoid having to buy new cassettes, he played songs on his tape deck that were no longer on anybody's hit parade. To avoid having to hire an assistant during school vacations, he got rid of the brass rings hanging from the carousel roof and the wooden sticks the children used to snag them. (That also eliminated the lollipops for the winners.)

He felt a certain pleasure in punishing the TV-addicted kids of today, who were more and more spoiled, less and less innocent, and who no longer dreamed of spinning merry-go-rounds with wooden horses and gilt carriages!

Maxime became melancholy and stingy. He armored himself with his bitterness.

For the thirteenth night in a row, young Omar-Paul walked around the carousel.

In between classes the boy, wide-eyed and mesmerized, watched it turning. He dreamed of taking a ride on it. But he hadn't a centime in his pocket, and the grumpy-looking owner certainly wouldn't give him a ride on credit.

Enchanted by the capering horses, Omar-Paul swayed in time to the music. The gleaming carriage, its door ajar as though in welcome, beckoned to him, but immediately brought to mind his own old home, what little there was left of it, blasted to pieces by the bombs!

The young boy watched the passersby as they sauntered across the square, unaware of the pleasures around them, unconscious even of the simple joy of coming and going without risking death at every street corner.

The painful memory of his native city, which he had left several months before, filled his mind.

Here, tall trees stood next to solid buildings. There, whole blocks lay in ruins. Broken tree trunks filled crevasses, and collapsed apartment buildings lay shattered, their walls riddled with bullets.

Some of those bullets had made him an orphan. Another had passed through his cheek. A third went through his shoulder, tearing off his left arm.

Some elderly, childless cousins who had long lived on the banks of the Seine took Omar-Paul in. He was street smart and worldly wise. His relatives were busy, hardworking small business people, and they gave him complete freedom.

As soon as he arrived, they showed him around the neighborhood.

"You'll find everything you need right here. No need to go farther afield."

He asked about the strange, lonely tower in the square. His cousin, who prided himself on knowing a lot of history, explained.

"In the past, soldiers from all over Europe gathered in this square. Then they set out together to reconquer the Holy Land and spread the good word."

"Which good word?" asked the boy.

He himself had two books of good words: the Bible from his mother and the Koran from his father. Their union had caused a lot of trouble for his family. Omar-Paul came to his own conclusions very early on, and they made him both tolerant and skeptical. His own dual name bore witness to an alliance. He was determined to maintain its symbolism proudly and defiantly.

"God's word," his cousin replied.

Omar-Paul could guess at other bloody events behind those harsh words, other scenes of carnage and atrocities like those happening right then in his own country to people of all faiths. Suddenly, he began to shake all over.

"God isn't a killer!" he screamed.

"What's the matter with you? What's wrong?"

His relatives couldn't get another word out of him. Lips sealed, body stiff, Omar-Paul lapsed into silence for the rest of the day.

Thirteen nights later, standing in front of the carousel, he remembered that conversation.

Terrible scenes from his shattered city rose before his eyes. Once again, he saw familiar, well-loved faces suddenly metamorphose into hideous grimacing masks.

Like his parents, Omar-Paul was determined not to choose, not to hate. But his father and mother were dead—both of them, like so many others. Dead and buried!

Those memories, which nobody here could share, were so painful, he just wanted to stifle his sobs and find somewhere to hide.

That's when he thought of the carriage on the carousel. He would curl up in there. He would snuggle up on its padded velvet seat, as soft as his mother's breast.

Omar-Paul figured out where it was. He lifted a corner of the canvas cover and slipped into the gleaming carriage with a sigh of relief.

Once hidden inside, he took off his shoes.

Curled up and rocked by the carriage's springs like a baby in its cradle, he gradually fell asleep.

Maxime showed up early the next morning.

The days seemed long and tiresome. A series of chores awaited him: pull the canvas cover off and carefully fold it, oil the machinery, polish the mirrors, clean the wooden horses, make the carriage shine. Dust got into everything, and he had to do battle with it every twenty-four hours.

Should he think about retiring? Maxime pushed the idea away. What would he do with his free time? How would he repay the debts he had incurred to buy and renovate the merry-go-round equipment?

As he neared the square, the carousel owner glared at the tower, standing alone and unattached to any church.

He would have liked to go into a chapel, dip his hand in the font, and dab holy water on his forehead, his lips, his heart.

The sight of the meaningless steeple—the bell tower with no bell and the useless spire—made him all the more irritable.

He lifted the cover with precise, impatient movements, then gave a sudden cry.

He had just found a little boy curled up inside the carriage, a long-haired boy startled awake by his shout.

With a bound, Maxime leapt to the carriage door and yanked it open. He grabbed the sleepy urchin's one arm and dragged him out.

"Out!" he yelled. "Out!"

Gradually gathering his wits, the boy tried to protest his innocence.

"I came to take a ride. There was no one here."

"Take a ride? In the middle of the night?"

"At home, it's always night!" he retorted.

"Home? Where's that?"

That was one question Omar-Paul wouldn't answer. Certain places can't be described. Naming them only increases the feeling of isolation and abandonment caused by ignorant people's indifference.

Maxime broke the silence.

"I don't give a damn where you come from! One thing's for sure: looking the way you do, with no shoes on your feet"—he didn't dare mention the missing arm—"I'd never let you ride on my carousel!"

"My shoes are in your carriage," the boy shot back. "And you better give them to me!"

"Get rid of them, you mean. You and your vermin."

"Vermin? I don't have any. Never have. Look." He

shook his abundant black curls. "You tell me if you find a single louse in my hair."

"Beat it or I'll call the police!"

The child wasn't frightened by these threats. In one glance, he had taken the measure of the man. Behind his swearing and irritability, the man was fragile, sensitive, even compassionate. Because of all he had lived through in his ravaged country, Omar-Paul had learned very early to size people up accurately. This judgment of life and its precariousness made him both patient and adaptable.

"Why 'I don't give a damn'? Why 'beat it'? Why 'police'? Why do you use these words against me?"

Standing on tiptoe, the child tried to look his interlocutor in the eye.

"Don't get angry. Use me. You won't regret it!"

"Use you? What good are you to me, with only one arm?"

"First: by helping you, I can pay for my night in the carriage. Second: I'll clean your carousel, turn it into a jewel. Third: I'm offering you my services for free."

Sensing that he had hit a vulnerable spot, Omar-Paul insisted, "Did you hear me? For free!"

Before Maxime had time to reply, the child grabbed the rags, feather duster, broom, and cleaning products and set to work rubbing, brushing, and polishing, humming all the while.

Using his one arm and his two strong legs, he climbed onto the roof of the carousel to polish its scarlet dome.

"What a monkey!" Maxime exclaimed, half admiring, half contemptuous.

"Quick as a monkey," the child responded, turning the expression to his advantage.

A few minutes later, he was standing in front of Maxime again.

"I can also put on an act for you."

"An act?"

"I make people laugh. Laugh till they cry!"

Omar-Paul stumbled over this last word. It brought back too many real horrors, too much real grief. Then he started again.

"Laugh till their sides ache. Give me some paint and some pieces of cloth, and you'll see."

He ducked into the shed. Squeezed in between the sound system, the machinery, and the cash register, he got dressed up and painted his face.

Maxime felt vaguely suspicious, but he pushed the feeling away. Since the boy had appeared, he had been filled with contradictory thoughts that swung between sympathy and rejection.

His curiosity aroused, he decided to play along. Feeling as impatient as an audience waiting for the curtain to go up, he found himself looking forward to the odd little urchin's reappearance.

When Omar-Paul presented himself, he had scarlet hair and a multicolored face, his eyes and mouth accented with orange paint. The carousel owner stared at him, open-mouthed.

A feather duster in place of the missing arm made the boy look like some exotic creature, half human, half bird. He hopped along pigeon-toed, hips swaying, tongue darting out of his mouth and lapping the air.

Maxime burst out laughing.

"What a clown!"

Fascinated by Omar-Paul's clown show, the crowds soon started to come. Dragging the adults after them, children in droves flocked to the carousel and stayed there until closing time.

At the end of the day, Maxime and the boy would replace the heavy canvas cover. The tasks and games had brought them closer.

After a week, Maxime congratulated the boy and asked him what his name was.

"Omar-Paul."

"Omar-Paul? Those two names don't go together at all!"

"My name is Omar-Paul," the boy insisted.

"We need to find something else."

"Don't you touch my name!" he retorted sharply

His tone was curt. Despite the boy's easygoing nature, Maxime sensed that he could put up an impenetrable wall against anything that threatened him.

"I didn't mean to hurt your feelings."

"You could add a third name to my first two," the boy replied, suddenly conciliatory.

"A third name? What name would that be?"

"Chaplin! Call me Omar-Paul Chaplin."

The little boy worshipped the great Charlie Chaplin. The Little Tramp had been mistreated by people and events, as he had; had been overwhelmed by catastrophe, as he had; and had known how to swiftly ward off disaster with mime, clowning, and laughter, as he had.

"Chaplin? You really think it's a good idea?" Maxime didn't feel this cosmopolitanism boded well.

"It's a great idea. It'll bring you lots of money."

Omar-Paul had an innate sense of business. Since antiquity, his ancestors had been sailing, trading, and establishing profitable trading posts on every shore of the Mediterranean.

"Put up posters all around the square with my name in big letters."

"What about your family? You have a family, don't you? What will they think of all this? I need this to be legit. I don't want any trouble."

Omar-Paul would deal with his family! He would explain to them that the carousel owner would start paying him once he learned the ropes. He would also promise to go to night school. Preoccupied by their business, his cousins would be relieved to learn that the child, traumatized by the war and the loss of his parents, had found a job he enjoyed.

"Clown!" "Charlie Chaplin!" With his silly-looking face, his pigeon-toed walk, and his feather-duster wing beating time, Omar-Paul would make people laugh.

Laughter, bursts of laughter would be a response to the madness of men and the absurdity of death.

"I know what you're thinking," grumbled Maxime. "Soon you'll be demanding a salary."

"Free!" the child reassured him. "You pay for the posters, you give me rides on the carousel, and I'll do the rest—for free."

"Okay then," said Maxime, satisfied with this response. "For free."

Had the kid possessed him? Or was it the other way round? Maxime shrugged. The encounter had given him back his zest for life.

Soon the poster was ready. The boy had chosen the font, style, and colors. OMAR-PAUL CHAPLIN stood out in red capital letters.

Omar-Paul ran around the carousel, joking, dancing, and fooling around. But suddenly his comedy act would disintegrate, as if it had hit an invisible wall. At those moments, he'd utter rambling, disconnected words, which he punctuated by waving his stump. With short, sharp sentences and gestures, he would evoke pillage, massacre, and sorrow.

Then, just as suddenly, the child would recover, hiding the horror behind pirouettes and buffoonery.

Now standing upright on the white horse, now flat on his back on one of the roan ones, now popping out of the carriage like a devil, Omar-Paul whirled from one part of the carousel to another.

The children kept flocking to him. The parents paid up without complaint.

Business was booming. Maxime bought the latest CDs, and he turned on the little light bulbs before it got dark. He even considered handing out lollipops again.

One afternoon, he sat down in the carriage. Relaxing as he was rocked and spun around, he whistled a popular tune. He felt happy.

The mothers and the babysitters started looking

younger. Maxime offered a free ride on the white horse to one woman's little boy. She was a brunette with a melancholy gaze, who wore brightly colored dresses, and whom he had nicknamed "the Scarlet Poppy." He hoped his generosity might help him win her over later.

In August, Omar-Paul's cousins went to Auvergne on vacation, so Maxime fixed up a bed for the boy at his place. Neither of them considered closing down the merry-go-round.

Soon, the carousel owner got to thinking about getting a prosthetic arm for the little boy. He took him to an orthopedist and paid for the visit. When Omar-Paul tried on the new arm, it was a decisive moment.

Maxime once again became generous and lively. He invited the Scarlet Poppy to dinner. That evening, he was happy to learn that she was divorced. The boy she took care of wasn't hers, but the son of a girlfriend she helped on weekends.

"My name is Madeleine."

Two years slipped by like that. Two glorious years!

Madeleine came over every evening. The carousel glittered with a thousand lights. Omar-Paul Chaplin's reputation had spread along both banks of the Seine.

"I'll be away all day today," Maxime announced one winter morning.

"Where are you going?"

"That's my secret."

He added with a wink, "I'll tell you some day, Omar-Paul."

By eight o'clock that night, Maxime still hadn't come

back. It was getting chilly in the square. There was no one at the carousel apart from Madeleine. The young woman helped Omar-Paul put the canvas cover on, then they both took shelter in the shed.

Frost gradually spread over the deserted square.

Soon it was nine o'clock, then eleven o'clock, then midnight.

The anxious woman and child rushed to Maxime's apartment, but he wasn't there. They looked everywhere but couldn't find an envelope or a message.

The hours of waiting were followed by frantic calls to hospitals and police stations.

The next morning, they learned that a slightly drunk Maxime had been run over by a car in the Place de la Concorde.

They found him in an intensive care unit, in traction, with tubes running everywhere. His breathing was ragged.

"The poor man, he's delirious," the nurse whispered, "He keeps calling for Chaplin. You know, Charlie Chaplin."

After three days, Maxime recognized the boy. Omar-Paul and Madeleine, whose fuchsia dress lit up the grayish walls, were holding hands. The doctor had warned them that there was no hope of saving the carousel owner.

Just the same, Maxime was smiling and moving his lips. Omar-Paul leaned close to listen.

"Now you have four names . . ."

"Rest, Maxime. You shouldn't tire yourself out."

"Let me . . . speak," he murmured.

"Listen to him," said Madeleine. Her hand in the child's was trembling. "Please, listen to him."

"Now you're called Omar-Paul Chaplin-Balin." The dying man forced each word out as he drifted into unconsciousness.

He came out of the coma several times over the next hour, and repeated, "Free of charge, free, FREE!" like some catchy refrain.

For the last time, Maxime and Omar-Paul exchanged their password, "Free, free, FREE!" they echoed.

A week later, Omar-Paul learned from the notary that the carousel owner had legally adopted him.

He'd been working on it for months.

On the day the process was complete, Maxime had stopped at a bar to celebrate the happy event. Under his arm he was carrying a magnum of champagne to celebrate with Madeleine and the little boy.

The broken bottle had been found beside him, its airy, sparkling bubbles slowly mixing with the flow of blood.

Translated by Anna Livia

The Grape Harvest

Colette

I HAD WRITTEN to my friend Valentine: "Come, they'll be harvesting the grapes." She came, wearing flat-heeled canvas shoes and an autumn-colored skirt; one bright-green sweater, and another pink one; one hat made of twill and another made of velvet, and both, as she said, "invertebrate." If she hadn't called a slug a snail, and asked if bats were the female of the screech owl, she wouldn't have been taken for "someone from Paris."

"Harvesting the grapes?" she asked, astonished. "Really? Despite the war?"

And I understood that deep down she was finding fault with all that the pretty phrase "harvesting the grapes" seems to promise and call forth of rather licentious freedom, singing and dancing, risqué intentions, and over-

COLETTE (1873–1954) was the author of many well-known novels, noted for their intimate style and sense of place. Widely translated into English, they include *The Complete Claudine*, *The Vagabond*, *Chéri*, *The Last of Chéri*, *Gigi*, and *Green Wheat*. "The Grape Harvest" was originally published in 1917 in *La vie parisienne* and was included in the posthumous collection *Paysages et portraits* (1958).

indulgence . . . Don't people traditionally refer to it as "the festival of the grape"?

"Despite the war, Valentine," I confessed. "What can you do? They haven't found a way of gathering the grapes without harvesting them. There are a lot of grapes. With the full-flavored grapes we'll make several casks of the wine that's drunk young and doesn't gain anything from aging, the wine that's as rough on the mouth as a swear word, and which the peasants celebrate the way people praise a boxer: 'Damn strong stuff,' being unable to find any other virtues in it."

The weather was so beautiful the day of the harvest, it was so enjoyable to dally along the way, that we didn't reach the hillside until around ten o'clock, the time when the low hedges and the shady meadows are still drenched in the blue and the cold of dripping dew, while the busy Limousin sun is already stinging your cheeks and the back of your neck, warming the late peaches under their cottony plush, the firmly hanging pears, and the apples, too heavy this year, which are picked off by a gust of wind. My friend Valentine stopped at the blackberries, the fuzzy teasel, even at the forgotten ears of maize whose dry husks she forced back and whose kernels she gobbled down like a little hen.

Like the guide in the desert, walking ahead and promising the lagging traveler the oasis and the spring, I cried out to her from a distance, "Come on, hurry up, the grapes are better, and you'll drink the first juice from the vat, you'll have bacon and chicken in the pot!"

Our entry into the vineyard caused no commotion. The work pressed on, and moreover, our attire warranted neither curiosity nor even consideration. My friend had agreed, in order to sacrifice herself to the blood of the grape, that I lend her an old checked skirt, which since 1914 had seen many other such sacrifices, and my personal adornments didn't go beyond an apron-smock made of polka-dot sateen. A few weather-beaten heads were raised above the cordons of vines, hands held out two empty baskets toward us, and we set to work.

Since my friend Valentine was thinning her bunches of grapes like an embroideress, with delicate snips of her scissors, it pleased a jovial and mute old faun, popping up opposite her, to give her something of a fright, and then silently show her how the clusters of grapes come off the stock and drop into the basket, if one knows how to pinch a secret suspension point, revealed to the fingers by a little abscess, a swelling where the stem breaks like glass. A moment later, Valentine was gathering the grapes, sans scissors, as quickly as her instructor the faun, and I didn't want her doing better or more than I, so the eleven o'clock sun wasted no time in moistening our skin and parching our tongues.

Whoever said grapes quench one's thirst? These Limousin grapes, grafted from American stock, so ripe they had split, so sweet they were peppery, staining our skirts, and being crushed in our baskets, inflamed us with thirst and intoxicated the wasps. Was my friend Valentine searching, when she straightened up to rest from time to time, was she searching the hillside, amid the well-regulated comings and goings of the empty and full baskets, for the child cupbearer who might bring an earthen jar filled with cool water? But the children carried only bunch after bunch of grapes, and the men—three old caryatids with muscles bared—transported only purple-stained tubs toward the gaping storeroom of the farm at the bottom of the hill.

The exuberance of the pure morning had gone away. Noon, the austere hour when the birds are silent, when the shortened shadow crouches at the foot of the tree. A cope of heavy light crushed down on the slate roofs, flattened out the hillside, smoothed out the shady fold of the valley. I watched the sluggishness and melancholy of midday descend over my energetic friend. Was she looking around her, among the silent workers, for a gaiety she might find fault in perhaps? Some relief—for which she didn't wait long.

A village clock was answered by a joyful murmuring, the sound of clogs on the hardened paths, and a distant cry:

"Soup's on! Soup's on! Soup's on!"

Soup? Much more and much better than soup, in the shelter of a tent made of reed thatch draped with ecru sheets, pinned up by twigs with green acorns, blue convolvulus, and pumpkin flowers. Soup and all its vegetables, yes, but boiled chicken too, and short ribs of beef, and bacon as pink and white as a breast, and veal in its own juices. When the aroma of this feast reached my friend's nose, she smiled that unconscious, expansive smile one sees on nurslings who have had their fill of milk and women who have had their fill of pleasure.

She sat down like a queen, in the place of honor, folded her purple-stained skirt under her, rolled back her sleeves, and cavalierly held out her glass to her neighbor to the right, for him to fill, with a saucy laugh. I saw by the look on her face that she was about to call him "my good man" . . . but she looked at him, kept quiet, and turned toward her neighbor to the left, then toward me as though in need of help and advice . . . As it was, country protocol had seated her between two harvesters who between them carried, slightly bent under such a weight, a hundred and sixty-six years. One was thin, dried up, pellucid, with bluish eyes and impalpable hair, who lived in the silence of an aged sprite. The other, still a giant, with bones fit for making clubs, single-handedly cultivated a piece of land, boasting ahead of time, in defiance of death, about the asparagus he'd get out of it "in four or five years"!

I saw the moment when Valentine, between her two old men, began losing her cheerfulness, and I had a liter of cider taken to her by a page who was just the sort to distract her, one of those beaming boys a little ungainly for their sixteen years—with a submissive and deceitful forehead, brown eyes, and a nose like an Arab—and every bit as handsome as the hundred-times-praised shepherds of Italy. She smiled at him, without paying him much attention, for she was in the grip of a statistical preoccupation. She asked the wispy old man, then the powerful octogenarian, their ages. She leaned forward to learn that of another frizzy-haired and wrinkled laborer who only admitted to seventy-three years. She gathered still other figures known to all from the far ends of the table—sixty-eight and seventy-one—began muttering to herself, adding up lustra and centuries, and was laughed at by a strapping young wench five times a mother, who shouted to her from where she sat: "Say, then, you like 'em like wine, huh, with cobwebs on the cork!"—provoking cracked laughter and young laughter, remarks in dialect and in very clear French as well, which made my friend blush and renewed her appetite. She wanted some more bacon, and cut into the peasant bread, made of pure wheat, brown but succulent, and demanded from the gnarled giant an account of the war of 1870. It was brief.

"What's to say? It wasn't a very pretty sight ... I remember everybody falling all around me and dying in their own blood. Me, nothin' ... not a bullet, not a bayonet. I was left standing, and them on the ground ... who knows why?"

He fell into an indifferent silence, and the faces of the women around us darkened. Until then, no mother deprived of her sons, no sister accustomed to double work without her brother, had spoken of the war or those missing, or groaned under the weariness of three years ... The farmer's wife, tight-lipped, busied herself by setting out thick glasses for the coffee, but she said nothing of her son, the artilleryman. One gray-haired farmer, very tired, his stomach cinched up with a truss, said nothing about his four sons: one was eating roots in Germany, two were fighting, the fourth was sleeping beneath a machine-gunned bit of earth ...

From a very old woman, seated not far from the table on a bundle of straw, came this remark: "All this war, it's the barons' fault ..."

"The barons?" inquired Valentine with great interest. "What barons?"

"The barons of France," said the cracked voice. "And

them of Germany! All the wars are the fault of the barons."

"How's that?"

My friend gazed at her avidly, as if hoping that the black rags would fall, and that the woman would rise up, a wimple on her head, her body in squirrel fur, croaking, "I, I am the fourteenth century!" But nothing of the kind happened, the old woman merely shook her head, and all that could be heard were the drunken and confident wasps, the puffing of a little train off in the distance, and the mawing gums of the pellucid old man . . .

Meantime, I had broken the maize *galette* with my hands, and the tepid coffee stood in the glasses, which the harvesters were already turning away from, back toward the blazing hillside . . .

"What," said Valentine, astonished, "no siesta?"

"Yes, of course! But only for you and me. Come over under the hazelnut trees, we can let ourselves melt away, ever so gently, with heat and sleep. The grape harvest isn't allowed the siesta that goes with the wheat harvest. There they are already back at work, look . . ."

But it wasn't true, for the ascending column of men and women had just halted, attentive . . .

"What are they looking at?"

"Someone's coming through the field . . . two ladies. They're waving to the harvesters . . . They know them. Did you invite any of your country neighbors?"

"None. Wait, I think I know that blue dress. Why . . . Why, it's . . ."

"They're . . . Why, yes, of course!"

Unhurried, coquettish, one beneath a straw hat, the

other beneath a white parasol, our two maids moved
toward us. Mine was swinging, above two little khaki-
colored kid shoes, a blue serge skirt which set off the
saffron-colored lawn of her blouse. My friend's soubrette,
all in mauve, was showing her bare arms through her
openwork sleeves, and her belt, made of white suede like
her shoes, gripped a waist which fashion might perhaps
have preferred less frail . . .

From our hideaway in the shade, we saw ten men run
up to them, and twenty hands hail them on the steep
slope, while envious little girls carried their parasols for
them. The aged giant, suddenly animated, sat one of the
maids down on an empty tub and hoisted the whole thing
onto his shoulder; a handsome, suntanned adolescent
smelled the handkerchief he had snatched from one of the
two young women. The heavy air seemed light to them,
now that two women's laughter, affected, deliberately pro-
longed, had set it in motion . . .

"They've gone to considerable expense, heavens!" murmured my friend Valentine. "That's my mauve Dinard
dress from three years ago. She's redone the front of the
bodice . . ."

"Really?" I said in a low voice. "Louise has on my serge
skirt from two years ago. I would never have believed it
could look so fresh. You could still find magnificent serge
back then . . . The devil if I know why I ever gave her my
yellow blouse! I could use it on Sundays this year . . ."

I glanced involuntarily at my polka-dot apron-smock,
and I saw that Valentine was holding, between two contemptuous fingers, my old checked skirt, covered with
purple stains. Above us, on the roasting hillside, the

mauve young woman and the yellow one were walking amid flattering laughter and happy exclamations. The elegance, the Parisian touch, the chatelaine's dignity, of which we had deprived the grape harvest, were no longer missing, thanks to them, and the rough workers once again became gallant, youthful, audacious, for them . . .

A hand, that of a man kneeling, invisible, between the vine stocks, raised a branch laden with blue grapes up to our maids, and both of them, rather than fill any basket, plucked off what pleased them.

Then they sat down on their unfolded handkerchiefs on the edge of a slope, parasols open, to watch the harvesting of the grapes, and each harvester rivaled the other in ardor before their benevolent idleness.

Our silence had lasted a long time, when my friend Valentine broke it with these words, unworthy, to be sure, of the great thought they expressed: "What I say is . . . bring back feudalism!"

Translated by Robert Phelps

Garcinets Pass

Pierre Magnan

DO YOU KNOW GARCINETS PASS? The road over it is so marginal, so indistinct and pointless, that the cartographer responsible almost didn't bother putting it on the map.

The road runs from Selonnet to Turriers and Bellaffaire, and it's laced with tortuous turns that bend over backward whenever they encounter the area's few torrents. The road can't seem to decide whether to follow them or cross them, just like the men who figured out the cheapest way to build it—following a mule track that for a thousand years was the only way to get into this godforsaken but magnificent part of the country.

The road cuts through crystals formed in fire fifteen

PIERRE MAGNAN (1922–) writes books deeply rooted in his native Provence. He published his first novel, *L'aube insolite*, at twenty-four, then spent decades writing on the side until scoring with *Le sang des Atrides* (1978), the first of his many detective stories. Six years later Magnan wrote his best-known book, *La maison assassinée* (1984, tr. *The Murdered House*). "Garcinets Pass" is from chapter 1 of *Le parme convient à Laviolette* (2000), a mystery set in the mountainous backcountry north of Nice.

million years ago, when the Pyrenees were casually spreading out and the Alps rose up to block their path. In the geological Gordian knot produced by that huge collision, the rock solidified into shards resembling long slivers of dead wood that look like so many sharpened daggers.

When only the moon and stars look down on Garcinets Pass, they're reflected in millions of those daggers, and they tumble down the glittering water courses, illuminating the close, stream-whispering darkness like a riot of paper lanterns.

If you've never seen Garcinets Pass on a heavy November day with black clouds cascading silently out of a sky that threatens rain, you don't know what loneliness is. Around here, three vehicles a day pass by: the milk truck making its pickups; the Seyne baker, who delivers as far as Bellaffaire; and the mailman in his yellow truck, who doesn't linger in these forbidding surroundings.

As it happens, there was also a man on a bicycle on one mid-autumn night in the year such-and-such. He was on his way to Bellaffaire to slaughter a pig for the Bardouin family at la Varzelle. The farm was a prosperous one in this land of poor people because the Bardouins had always *fait petit*. In our parts, *faire petit* means to be economical in the extreme. When a mother—if she's a good mother—sees her child wolfing down a sandwich, she'll shout, "*Fais petit!*"

It means keep your appetite in check, tell yourself you have more to eat and more time to enjoy it. It means make your pleasure last.

For the Bardouin dynasty, that command applied in

spades. In three generations of stinginess, they'd acquired an extraordinary ability to say no to everyone. In the course of three centuries, *faire petit* had become their dominant gene.

La Varzelle was on the flank of the Bardonnache valley, which is walnut country. There were at least sixty of those spreading trees, planted along fields and bordering plots, sometimes towering over the country roads, their trunks rising straight and free of knots for thirty feet. Around here, nobody who owned sixty smooth-trunked walnut trees was ever said to have died poor.

The man on his bicycle panted as he cut the tortuous pass's curves, busy listing the reasons the Bardouins had to consider themselves rich. He himself was poor, and even though he'd done a lot of rolling, he'd never been able to gather any moss.

Yet, he had been of service to so many people! After joining the Resistance in 1943 at sixteen, he'd accepted all the dangerous missions that the Maquis leaders ordered but wouldn't go on themselves. He'd been recognized as a hero with some surprise: he should have been killed a dozen times, but survived. Still, they gave him a medal that he wore on important memorial days, where the survivors of the last couple of wars are lumped together so as to impinge on the workweek as little as possible.

He had some good memories, anyway. Before his prestige as a hero vanished along with his waistline, a few women had loved him. To spur on his pedaling, he now summoned the images and the words left in his memory when they'd embraced him and thanked him, more or less convincingly.

The man's name was Ferdinand Bayle, and as he struggled up Garcinets Pass in the wavering beam of his headlight that evening, he didn't get much comfort from those memories, because he had deep wrinkles and a head like a loaf of bread, and also because at fifty, he was alone.

He was a poor man who got by on little: a few days' work here and there, a few snares to catch the thrushes that alighted on others' fields in the fall. Oh, and also a small harvest from *rabasse* truffle grounds that belonged to people who died without heirs. Those people had been carefully watched, while they were alive, when they kneeled as if in prayer and waved their hazel branch like a conductor's baton over the truffle flies. Those people's movements had been studied as they held the stick horizontally, like a sextant, following the flies' vertical dance directly over the patch of bare ground where the truffle was hiding. Bayle had memorized the exact place and those movements, adding hundreds more from here and there, until the eulogy for the man he had spied on so carefully reached him.

"Chabrias is dead, too!"

Around here, that "too" means that this Chabrias had died *in addition* to all the other ones. So the next winter, you tiptoe in at sunset and pay obeisance at the foot of the rabasse oak tree until the fly with the golden wings came to dance above the truffle ground. Then, when you're sure of the spot, you quickly and carefully dig with the coffee scoop—found in some grocery store—cautiously burrowing with your fingers. In good years you can get 200, maybe 300 grams of misshapen truffles in a week.

They're misshapen because in our part of the country, the fickle rabasse would rather squeeze between a pair of stones than grow nice and round in soft dirt a few inches away. No one's yet been able to explain why our truffles choose to grow between two sharp stones. If we only knew that . . .

This was what the panting man thought as he climbed Garcinets Pass standing up on his pedals, accompanied by the clinking of the long butcher's sharpening steel that hung from his belt.

Bayle had all the time in the world to mull over the twists and turns of his mediocre existence, combining his erotic memories with those of clandestine truffle hunting. It didn't amount to a very full life, and at fifty, which he was then, there wasn't much hope of a change. With 350,000 kilometers on the odometer, his tractor was about to give up the ghost. When he would have to approach the Credit Agricole, the mouths of his fellow peasants on the board would tighten the moment they heard the word "loan." They knew he was unlucky and had no reason to think anything had changed.

"What can we say . . . ?"

That's what they would say, their outspread arms accentuating the ellipsis that ended the discussion.

"What can we say . . . ?" That scrap of speech meant, "You just don't have any luck! If you carefully pick the moment between two showers to cut your hay and bring it in, you're sure to make it rain—you're famous for it! Be honest: in the last twenty years, how many times have you brought in your hay dry?"

Only the lucky ones got loans, only the hard workers got loans, because the world, which fears bad luck, confuses bad luck with laziness.

The only thing that kept Bayle from being turned off his plot of land was the bad publicity it would bring the local officials. I ask you: what does a peasant turned off his land look like? A peasant who's had title to his land for maybe fifteen generations, who can't remember the exact date when his family acquired it? You'd have to rummage through the archives of four generations of notaries to find the original deed. No, you don't just dump him at the edge of his field with a few bundles and a couple of cages of chickens. It would look bad. Instead, you slip the file to the bottom of the stack and wait for better days.

But in the meantime, the tractor was breathing its last; Bayle was selling wheat on the sly (which everybody knew) so as not to go through the official organizations, which would take the money and not give any back; he was shearing his sheep six weeks early and feeding them hay because his barn was empty, even though new grass wouldn't come up for another three months. Was the haystack tall enough to feed the flock? Wouldn't he have to sell off the sheep at precisely the worst time of year, when the prices for animals are lowest because there isn't any grass?

Such was the complete picture of this unhappy man panting on a bicycle, one of whose wheels was probably out of true, since it was making a soft sound, like the beating of a wing, with every turn.

When Bayle died, his eulogy would be lifted from a police report. "Lived by his wits."

What else could you call that executioner's errand he was on: going to kill pigs for other people?

The pig is the animal that is closest to man. It feeds him, but it leaves him feeling guilty. You can kill a lamb or a calf with a clear conscience, but never a pig. Every evening, when the thick soup with its chunk of fatback is brought to the table, it's as if that year's pig were there, reminding you of its kindness. There are more than sixty dead pigs in the life of every Bas-Alpes peasant, and they all come to speak to you of their friendship, today and at the hour of your death, amen!

"Amen!" said Bayle between gritted teeth.

At that thought, he realized he had reached the top of the pass. Ahead of him, the constellation Virgo was sinking toward the horizon, washed out by the brightness of the waning moon. A bitter smell of holm oaks rose from the depths of the Grand Vallon below Champdarène.

The farm he was headed for could be seen below. They had lit all the lamps as a signal for him, like a beacon. He was expected. In the glow, clouds of steam rose from a cauldron set over a hot fire, where they would draw water to scald the skin.

Bayle breathed deeply. The road went downhill now. All he had to do was coast, braking in the turns.

He tightened the strap that held the sharpening steel to his belt. He should have a sheath for it, but the sheath was like the tractor, long out of service. Bayle had gotten into the habit of carrying it unsheathed. He had only to wedge it against his thigh to keep it from clinking, because if the animal to be sacrificed heard, it would start to howl and he wouldn't be able to do his job in peace.

Now that he was over the pass, the light from the Bardouins was no longer visible, and the waning moon lit up the pavement. The few lights of Bellaffaire twinkled in the distance, a treat after the steep climb through the dark woods along the hidden road.

Bayle was almost happy. The woman who ran the Bardouin household was well set up and he had the distinct impression that when she came to hire him for the job, she'd looked him over from head to foot with the eye of a connoisseur. Now that was a pleasant thought to entertain while you're between the two banks of a tough road, lost in an inky night made even more lugubrious by the moon. In a man's mind, a woman is a light that can guide you through these unforgiving parts. Even if the attention she pays you is misleading, it's still better than a Saint Christopher medal against the hazards of the dark road.

That's what Bayle was thinking as he coasted down the treacherous slope.

"I have to adjust my brakes one of these days," he thought.

He'd been telling himself the same thing about the same bicycle for years. It was no longer a matter of adjusting the brakes but of replacing them. The rubber of the pads was long gone, but Bayle had a lot of experience with neglect. He knew how to tame it, charm it, master it. As he speeded into a curve, he suddenly noticed that the moonlit pavement had a strange oily sheen. But he didn't have time to slow down. His front wheel slid sideways, and the rear wheel, bearing all its rider's weight, reared like a horse and threw him.

Aside from the instinctive cursing of someone who has

lost his balance, a bicycle with a man on it doesn't make much noise as it tumbles into a ravine, bouncing from rock to rock all the way to the bottom of the valley, leaving its rider wrapped heavily around the trunk of a pine tree.

The warped wheel, the one that sounded like a beating wing, continued to spin for a few seconds. Without the generator to power it, the headlight began to dim.

Translated by William Rodarmor

Villa Aurora

Jean-Marie Gustave Le Clézio

AURORA HAD STOOD, for all time, up there on the hill-top, half lost in the lush tangle of plants, yet still visible between the trunks of latania and palms, a great, white, cloud-colored palace quivering in the leafy shadows. It was called Villa Aurora even though no name had ever been inscribed on the pillars of the gateway, only a number engraved on a marble plaque that had worn away long before I could ever remember it. Perhaps it had been given the name precisely because of its cloudlike color, so like the faint, iridescent hue of sky at dawn's first break. But everyone knew about Aurora, and it was the first strange

JEAN-MARIE GUSTAVE LE CLÉZIO (1940–) is one of France's best-known contemporary writers. In more than twenty novels and nonfiction works he lends his voice to the dispossessed, exploring such themes as alienation, immigration, poverty, violence, and the loss of innocence. A small sampling of his books includes *Le procès-verbal* (1963), *La fièvre* (1975, tr. *Fever*), and *Le chercheur d'or* (1985, tr. *The Prospector*). "Villa Aurora" is from *The Round and Other Cold Hard Facts*, C. Dickson's translation of *La ronde et autres faits divers* (1982). She also translated Le Clézio's *Étoile errante* (1992, tr. *Wandering Star*).

house ever shown to me, the first house to etch itself on my memory.

I first heard about the lady of Villa Aurora around that same time, and I suppose she must have been pointed out to me on occasion as she was strolling down the garden paths in her large sun hat or trimming the rose bushes by the wall near the gateway. But my recollection of her is blurred, elusive, barely perceptible, so that I can't be altogether certain of having really seen her at all, and I sometimes wonder if I haven't imagined her instead. I often heard talk of her in conversations (between my grandmother and her friends mostly) that I listened to absentmindedly but in which she quickly stood out as an odd sort of person, a kind of fairy perhaps, whose very name seemed to be filled with mystery and promise: the lady of Villa Aurora. Because of the name, because of the pearly sheen of her house glimpsed through the undergrowth, because of the garden as well—so vast, so forsaken, in which a multitude of birds and stray cats dwelled—whenever I thought of her, whenever I neared her domain, a little adventurous thrill would run through me.

Later on, along with other mischief-makers, I learned how to enter that domain through a breach in the old wall, over by the gully on the shady side of the hill. But in those days we no longer talked of the lady of Villa Aurora or even of Villa Aurora itself. We spoke of them in periphrases that we had undoubtedly invented for purposes of exorcising the mystery of early childhood and justifying our trespassing. We would call it "going to the stray cats' garden" or else "going through the hole in the wall." But we were careful to stay in the wild part of the garden, the part where the cats lived, with their miraculous litters of blind kittens, and two or three plaster statues had been given over to the vegetation. During those games of hide-and-seek and reconnaissance expeditions through the jungle of acanthus and bay laurels, very rarely did I glimpse, remote and dreamlike, surrounded by the trunks of palms, the great white house with its fan-shaped stairway. And never once did I hear the voice of the mistress; never once did I see her on the stairs or on the gravel paths or even in a window.

Still, it's strange too when I think about those days— it's as if we all knew she was there, that she lived in the house, that this was her realm. Without even knowing what her real name was, we were aware of her presence; we were her familiars, her neighbors. There was a part of her that dwelled in the place, up there on that hilltop back then. Something that we couldn't really see but that was present in the trees, in the palms, in the shape of the white house, in the two stone pillars of the gateway, and in the high, rusty gate chained shut. It was like the presence of something from olden times, something very gentle and remote, the presence of the old gray olive trees, of the giant, lightning-scarred cedar, of the old walls encircling the place like ramparts. It was also in the odor of the dusty bay laurels, in the clusters of pittosporum and orange trees, in the dark rows of the cypresses. Day after day, it was all there, without fail, never changing; and because she was at the core of it all, we were happy, without knowing it, without even intending to be.

We liked the cats a lot, too. Sometimes some of the brats would pursue them, throwing stones, but once they were through the breach in the wall, the hunt was off. There in the garden, inside the walls, was the home of the cats, and they knew it. They lived in packs of hundreds, clinging to the rocks on the shady side of the hill or half hidden in the hollows of the old wall, warming themselves in the pale winter sunlight.

I knew them well, all of them, just as if I'd known their names: the one-eyed white tomcat with battle-torn ears, the ginger cat, the black cat with azure eyes, the black and white cat with perpetually dirty paws, the golden-eyed gray she-cat and all her children, the bobtail cat, the tabby cat with a broken nose, the cat that looked like a small tiger, the angora cat, the white she-cat with her three kittens, all white like their mother. They were all famished, terrified, with dilated pupils, their coats grimy or shaggy; and then there were all those bound for death, teary-eyed, runny-nosed, so thin you could see their ribs and backbones through the fur. They all lived in the lovely mysterious garden, as though they were the creatures of the lady of Villa Aurora. For that matter, whenever we would venture near the garden paths, closer to the house, we'd see little piles of food set out on bits of wax paper or on old enamel plates. It was she who fed them, and they alone could approach her, could speak with her. People said she poisoned the food she gave them to put them out of their misery, but I don't think that was true; it was just another story concocted by people who didn't know Aurora and were afraid of her. And so we didn't dare go very near the paths or the walls, as if we belonged to another species, as if we should remain forever strangers.

I loved the birds as well because they were low-flying

blackbirds, hopping from tree to tree. They whistled funny, mocking tunes, perched on the topmost branches of the laurels or in the dark crowns of the araucaria. Sometimes I would play at answering them, whistling because it was the only place that you could hide in the underbrush and whistle like a bird without anyone barging in on you. There were robins too, and every so often near evening time, when darkness was settling upon the garden, a mysterious nightingale would sing his heavenly melody.

There was also something very peculiar in the vast, abandoned garden: it was a kind of circular temple, consisting of tall columns topped with a roof decorated with frescos, and on one side of it was written a mysterious word; it said:

ΟΥΡΑΝΟΣ

I would sit there for a long time, half hidden by the tall weeds, looking through the leaves of the bay laurels at the strange word without understanding. It was a word that took you a long way back, to another time, to another world, like the name of some imaginary land. There was no one in the temple except the blackbirds, which would sometimes hop about on the white marble steps and the wild grasses and vines that gradually overran the columns, entwining them, darkening them in places. In the waning light of dusk there was something even more mysterious about the place; it was due to the play of shadows on the marble steps and to the temple's peristyle, where the magic letters shone out. At the time, I believed the temple was real, and I sometimes went there with other neighborhood children—with Sophie, with Michael, with Lucas—crawling noiselessly through the weeds to contemplate it. But not one of us would have dared to venture onto the steps of the temple for fear of breaking the spell hanging over the place.

Later on—but by then I wasn't going to Aurora's garden anymore—later on someone explained to me what the temple really was, built by some nut who thought he was back in ancient Greece, and even explained the magical word, telling me how to pronounce it "ouranos," and said it meant "heaven" in Greek. He had learned all that in school, and he was certainly very proud of himself, but by then I couldn't have cared less; I mean it was all locked up in my memory already and nothing could change it.

The days were long and bright back then in the garden of Villa Aurora; there was nothing else of any interest in the town or the streets or the hills or even the sea, which we could glimpse off in the distance between the trees and the palms. In winter the garden was dreary and dripping with rain, but it was fine all the same to sit leaning up against a palm tree, for instance, and listen to the drumming of the rain on the great fronds and on the laurel leaves. The air would be still then, frozen, not a bird call or the sound of an insect to be heard. Night fell quickly, heavily, filled with secrets, carrying with it the acrid taste of smoke, and like a breeze blowing over the pond, the damp shadows came rippling through the leaves of the trees over your skin.

Or else, just before summer, the harsh, biting sun would come out amid the high branches, scorching the little clearings near the eucalyptus trees. When the heat was at its peak, I would go slowly, creeping like a cat up to the door in the undergrowth, from where I could see the temple. This was the time when it was most beautiful: the blue, cloudless sky and the white stone of the temple so intense, so dazzling, I would have to shut my eyes. Then I'd look at the magical name, and with only that name, I'd be able to take off, like going to another land, like entering a world that didn't really exist yet. There would be nothing but the blank sky and the white stone, the tall white marble columns, and the chirping sound of summer insects, as though they made up the very sound of the light. I would sit for hours at a time on the threshold of that world, without really wanting to enter it, simply looking at those letters that said the magic word and feeling the power of the light and smells. Even today, I can still recall it, the pungent smell of laurel, of bark, of broken branches baking in the heat of sun, the smell of the red soil. It's more powerful than reality, and the light that I gathered at that moment in the garden still shines within me more clearly and more intensely than the light of day. Things shouldn't change.

After that, there was something like a huge void in my life, up until the time when I just happened to come upon the garden of Villa Aurora again—its wall, its barred gate, the tumble of bushes, the bay laurels, the old palms. Why had I one day stopped going through the breach in the wall, slipping through the brambles and lying in wait for bird calls, for the fleeting shapes of stray cats? It was as though I'd been cut off from childhood, from games, from secrets, from garden paths by some long illness and it had become impossible to make the two ends meet.

Where had the child in me gone? For years, he was even totally unaware of being cut off, struck with amnesia, forever banished to another world.

He no longer saw the garden, no longer thought about it. The magical word written on the pediment of the fake temple had been completely erased, wiped out of his memory. It was a meaningless word, simply a word that opened the door to another realm for those who gazed upon it, half hidden in the wall of leaves and branches, still as a lizard in the light. So when you no longer looked at it, when you stopped believing in it, the word would fade, lose its power, and become just like all the other words we look at without seeing—words written on walls, on the pages of newspapers, glittering over shop windows.

It was around this same time that the fellow who studied Greek told me one day, just like that, sort of matter-of-factly, that it meant "heaven," and it just hadn't mattered at all anymore. It had become an ordinary subject of conversation, if you know what I mean. Just a subject of conversation, hot air, vacuous.

Even so, I did go out of my way to see it all once again one Saturday just before exams (that was when I was beginning to study law). I'd left the neighborhood so long ago that I had a hard time finding the street, the one that climbed all the way to the top of the hill, right up to the wall of Villa Aurora. There were tall apartment buildings everywhere now; they'd cropped out in a disorderly fashion on the hillside, right up to its crest, huddling against one another on their great blacktop platforms. Most of the trees had disappeared, except one or two here and there that had probably gone unnoticed in the havoc that had swept over the land: olive trees, eucalyptuses, some orange trees, now lost in the sea of asphalt and concrete, seemed scrawny, drab, aged, on the brink of death.

I walked through the unfamiliar streets, and I was gradually seized with a sense of dread. There was an odd feeling about everything, something like apprehension or maybe a deeply repressed fear, not founded upon anything real, like an intimation of death. The sunlight streamed down over the fronts of the buildings, over the balconies, firing sparks in the vast plate glass windows. The mild autumn wind ruffled the hedge leaves and the foliage of the ornamental plants in the gardens of private residences, for now they were tame plants of garish colors with strange names that I had only recently learned—poinsettias, begonias, strelitzias, jacarandas. From time to time there were still, just like in the old days, mocking blackbirds that screeched after me, that hopped about in the grass of the traffic circles, and the shouts of children and the barking of dogs. But death was underlying everything, and I sensed that it was inevitable. It was coming from all sides at once, welling up from the ground, hanging along the overly wide streets, around the empty crossroads, in the barren gardens, hovering in the gray fronds of the old palms. It was a shadow, a reflection, an odor perhaps, an emptiness that pervaded everything.

So then I stopped walking for a moment to try and understand. Things were so different! The villas had disappeared, or else they had been repainted, enlarged, transformed. In places where there had once been gardens protected by high, moss-grown walls, there now towered vast, intensely white buildings of ten, eight, twelve stories on their grease-stained parking lots. Most disconcerting of all was that I could no longer recall my past. The present reality had suddenly erased all of childhood's memories, leaving only a painful sense of barrenness, of mutilation, a vague, blind anxiety cutting off past feelings from the present. And so, dispossessed, banished, betrayed, or perhaps simply excluded, I sensed an aura of death, an aura of emptiness surrounding the world. The concrete and the asphalt, the high walls, the grass and marigold median strips, the low garden walls with their nickel-plated fencing—all of it had form, was filled with a glimmer of apprehension, was laden with ill will. I had just realized that in straying, in ceasing to keep my gaze intent upon my world, I had betrayed it, had abandoned it to its mutations. I had looked away, and meanwhile things had been able to change.

Where was Aurora now? Hurriedly, I walked along the empty streets toward the crest of the hill. I could see the names of the buildings inscribed in gilt lettering on the marble frontispieces, pretentious and empty names, names tantamount to their facades, their windows, their balconies:

THE PEARL

THE GOLDEN AGE

GOLDEN SUN

THE RESEDAS

SUNNYSIDE TERRACES

I thought then of the magical word, the word that neither I nor anyone else ever pronounced, the word that could only be seen, the word engraved at the top of the fake Greek temple faced with stucco, the word that bore one away into the light, into the raw sky, beyond everything, to a place that didn't exist yet. Perhaps it was that word I'd been missing all these years of my adolescence, years I had spent far from the garden, from Aurora's house, from all the paths. Now my heart was beating faster, and something was oppressing me, bearing down at the very quick of me, a pain, a restlessness, for I knew I wouldn't find what I was seeking, that I would never again find it, that it had been destroyed, devoured.

Everywhere up on top of the hill were gutted gardens, ruins, gaping wounds dug into the earth. At the building sites, tall, threatening cranes loomed motionless, and trucks had left muddy tracks on the pavement. The buildings hadn't finished sprouting up yet. They were still growing larger, biting into the old walls, scraping the earth, unfolding sheets of asphalt, dazzling concrete grounds at their feet.

I squinted my eyes half shut against the light of the setting sun bouncing off all of the white facades. There were no more shadows now, no more secrets. Only the underground garages of the buildings, opening out their wide, black doors, revealing the dark passageways of their foundations.

Every now and then I would think I recognized a house, a wall, or perhaps even a tree, an old laurel that had survived the destruction. But it was like a reflection; it would light up in a flash and then fade away just as suddenly before I could even grasp it; and then all that remained were the desolate surface of the asphalt and the high walls barring the sky.

I wandered around for a long time on the crest of the hill in search of some trace, some clue. Evening began to fall; the light was growing murky and dim; the blackbirds were flying heavily between the buildings in search of a place to sleep. It was they who led me to Villa Aurora. All of a sudden, I saw it. I hadn't recognized it because it was below the level of the circular highway, so crunched down under its supporting wall in the crook of the curve that I saw only its terrace roof and its chimneys. How could I possibly have forgotten it? With my heart pounding, I crossed the highway, running between two cars; I walked up to the wire fence. It was Villa Aurora all right. I'd never seen it up so closely before, and most of all, I'd never imagined what it might look like seen from above, as if from a bridge. Then it struck me as looking sad, gray, forlorn, with its high, close-shuttered windows and the plaster stained with rust and soot, the stucco eaten away with old age and misfortune. It had lost that faint pearly color that had once made it seem ethereal when I spied on it from between the low laurel branches. It had lost its color of dawn. Now it was a lurid whitish-gray, the color of sickness and death, the color of wood in a cellar, and even the soft glow of dusk could not light it.

Yet now there was nothing to conceal or shelter it. The trees around it had vanished, except for two or three dejected, twisted, grimacing olive trees growing under the highway on either side of the old house. Looking closely, I discovered, one by one, each of the old trees—the palms, the eucalyptuses, the laurels, the lemon trees, the rhododendrons—each of the trees that I had known, that had been as close to me as human beings, something like giant friends whom I wouldn't have dared get very near to. Yes, they were there still; it was true: they existed.

But like Villa Aurora, now they were simply empty forms, shadows, very pale and lightweight, as though they were hollow inside.

I stood there very still by the highway for a long time, looking at the roof of the old house, at the trees, and the bit of garden that was left. Then I was seeing beyond it all, contemplating the image of my childhood, and I tried to make what I had once loved come back to life—it would come and then go, come back again, wavering, unclear, maybe even painful—an image of fervor and elation that burned my eyes and the skin of my face, that made my hands tremble. The twilight vacillated on top of the hill, blanketing the sky, then receding, throwing the ashen clouds into abrupt contrast. The town all around had suddenly stopped short. The cars were no longer driving along in their lanes, nor were the trains or the trucks moving on the loops of the expressways. The highway behind me crossed over what had once been the garden of Villa Aurora, making a long curve almost suspended in mid-sky. But not a single car passed on the highway, not one. Before disappearing, the last light of the sun held the world spellbound, in suspense, for a few more minutes. My heart racing, face burning, I tried as quickly as possible to get back to the world I had loved; with all my might I tried to make it appear quickly—everything I had been, those hollows in the trees, those tunnels under the shadowy leaves, and the scent of the moist earth, the crickets' songs, the secret passageways of wild cats, their dens under the laurels, the white wall of Villa Aurora, light as a cloud, and most of all the temple, remote and mysterious as an airborne balloon, with on its front the word that I could see but that I couldn't read.

For a brief moment, the smell of burning leaves came, and I thought I was going to be able to go in, that I was going to find the garden once again and along with the garden, Sophie's face, the voices of children at play, my body, my arms and my legs, my independence, my path. But the smell died away; the twilight grew dull as the sun disappeared behind the clouds clinging to the hilltops. And then, everything came apart. Even the cars began moving again on the highway, taking the curve at high speed, and the sound of their motors fading into the distance tore me with pain.

I saw the wall of Villa Aurora, so close now that, had it not been for the wire fence along the highway, I could almost have touched it by stretching out my arm. I could see every detail of the wall—the streaked, flaking plaster, the stains of mildew around the drainpipes, spatters of tar, the scars left by machines when the highway had been built. The shutters of the high windows were closed now, but closed as though they would never again need to be opened, closed in the tight-lidded manner of the blind. On the grounds around the house, weeds had grown amid the gravel, and the beds of acanthus were overflowing everywhere, smothering the woodbine and the old orange trees. There was not a sound; nothing moved in the house. But it wasn't the silence of times past, laden with magic and mystery. It was an oppressive, awkward muteness that tightened in my chest and throat and gave me the urge to flee.

Still, I couldn't bring myself to leave. I walked alongside the fence now, trying to catch the slightest sign of life in the house, the slightest whisper. A little farther on, I saw the old, green-painted gate, the one I had once looked upon with a kind of awe, as if it had been shielding the entrance to a castle. It was the same gate, but the supporting pillars had changed. Now they were on the edge of the highway, two cement pillars already gray with soot. The beautiful number engraved on the marble plaque was no longer there. Everything seemed cramped, sad, shrunken with old age. There was a doorbell button with a name written under it, covered with a piece of grimy plastic. I read the name:

MARIE DOUCET

It wasn't familiar to me because no one had ever called the old lady anything but the lady of Villa Aurora, but I understood, merely in seeing the name written under the pointless doorbell, that it was the woman I loved, the woman I'd spied on for so long from my hiding places under the laurels without ever really seeing her.

Just to have seen her name, and to have loved it immediately, the handsome name that matched my memories so well, made me rather happy, and the sensation of frustration and alienation I had felt in walking through my old neighborhood nearly disappeared.

For a second, I was tempted to ring the doorbell, without thinking, impulsively, simply to be able to behold the face of the woman I'd loved for so long. But that was impossible. So I left. I walked back down the empty streets, amid the tall buildings with their lighted windows, with their car-filled parking lots. There were no more birds in the sky, and the old stray cats had no place to live now. I too had become a stranger.

A year later, I was able to return to the hilltop. I'd thought about it constantly, and despite all the activity and futility of student life, deep down there was still that feeling of uneasiness in me. Why? I think that ultimately I'd never quite been able to get used to not being what I had been, the child who went through the breach in the wall and who'd found all those hiding places, and passageways there in the great wild garden among the cats and the insect calls. It had remained within me, alive deep down inside of me, despite all the wide world that had drawn me away.

Now I knew I could walk up to Villa Aurora, that I would ring the doorbell over Marie Doucet's name, and that I was finally going to be able to enter the white house with its closed shutters.

Oddly enough, now that I had a good reason to call at the villa—what with that extraordinary ad in which Miss Doucet offered a "room for a student (male or female) who will agree to look after the house and protect it"—now, more than ever, I dreaded going there, forcing my way in, entering that strange realm for the first time. What would I say? Would I be able to speak to the lady of Villa Aurora normally, without having my voice waver and my words become jumbled, without my eyes betraying my emotion and especially my memories, the awe and the desire of my childhood? I walked slowly along the streets toward the crest of the hill, not thinking about anything for fear of giving rise to too many doubts. My eyes stared at insignificant things—the dead leaves in the gutters, the steps of the shortcut scattered with pine needles, the ants, the flies drowsing, the discarded cigarette butts.

When I came up below Villa Aurora, I was again surprised at all the changes. In the last few months, construction on several new buildings had been completed, several new sites had been begun, several old villas demolished, gardens disemboweled.

But above all, it was the highway running its curve around Villa Aurora that filled me with a terrible feeling of emptiness and destitution. Cars slid quickly over the asphalt with a sort of whistling sound, then moved off, disappearing between the tall buildings. Sunlight glittered everywhere—on the all-too-new walls of the buildings, on the black tar, on the hulls of cars.

Where was that fair light of the old days, the light I would catch sight of between the leaves on the face of the fake temple? Even the shadows had changed now: great, dark pools at the foot of residences, geometrical shadows of lampposts and wire fencing, hard shadows of parked cars. I thought then of the faint shadows dancing between the leaves, the shadows of trees intertangling, of old laurels, of palms. All of a sudden I remembered the round splashes that the sun would make shining through the leaves of the trees and the gray clouds of mosquitoes. That was what I was looking for on the barren ground, and my eyes stung with the light. That which had remained deep within me for all these years and which now, in this frightful barrenness, in the glaring light of the present, was creating a sort of veil over my eyes, a light-headedness, a fogginess: the shade of the garden, the soft shadows of trees that heralded the dazzling apparition of the lovely, pearl-colored house, surrounded by its garden, its mysteries, and its cats.

I rang only once, briefly, perhaps secretly hoping to myself that no one would come. But after a moment, the door of the villa opened and I saw an old woman dressed like a peasant or like a gardener; she was standing in the doorway, her eyes squinting because of the bright light, and she was trying to see me. She didn't ask what I wanted or who I was, so I said between the bars of the gate, speaking loudly, "I'm Gérard Estève; I wrote to you about the ad for the room . . ."

The old lady continued to look at me without answering, then she smiled a little and said, "Just a minute; I'll go fetch the key; I'm coming," with her gentle and weary voice, and I realized that it hadn't been necessary to shout.

I'd never seen the lady of Villa Aurora before, and yet now I knew that this was the way I must always have imagined her. An old lady with a sun-baked face, with white, short-cropped hair, and clothing that had aged along with her, the clothing of a poor woman or a peasant, faded with sun and with time. It was all just like her handsome name, Marie Doucet.

By her side, I walked into Villa Aurora. I was intimidated, and I felt ill at ease because everything was so old, so fragile. I walked slowly into the house, not saying a word, almost holding my breath, with the old lady leading the way. I was going along a dark corridor when the door opened onto the sitting room, bursting with golden light, and through the windows of the French doors I saw the leaves of the trees and the palms motionless in the dazzling light, as though the sun need never fade. And as I entered the large, timeworn room, it seemed to me that the walls opened out infinitely and that the house expanded, spread out over the whole of the hill, obliterating everything around it—the buildings, the roads, the deserted parking lots, the concrete chasms. Then I regained my size of old, the size I never should have lost, my child's proportions, and the old lady of Villa Aurora grew larger, lighted by the walls of her home.

My head was spinning so, I needed to steady myself on an armchair.

"What is it?" asked Marie Doucet. "Are you feeling ill? Would you like some tea?"

I shook my head, a little ashamed of my weakness, but the old lady was already going out of the room, answering herself, "Yes, yes I just happen to have the water heating; I'll be right back, have a seat there . . ."

Then we drank the tea in silence. My dizziness had disappeared, but I was still filled with that feeling of boundlessness, and I couldn't say a word. I just listened to the old lady talking, telling all about the adventures of the house, probably the last adventure she was living.

"They've come here; they'll come back, I know it; that's why I wanted a helper—I mean, someone like yourself to help me to—I did want a young lady; I thought that it would be best for her and for myself, but in the end, you know, there were two that came here; they looked over the house, they politely bid me good-bye, and I never saw them again. They were afraid; they didn't want to stay here.

I can understand how they felt; even if everything seems calm now, I know that they'll come back; they'll come in the night, and they'll bang on the shutters with their iron bars, and they'll throw rocks and give wild shouts. They've been doing that for years now, to frighten me, you understand, to make me leave here, but where would I go? I've always lived in this house; I wouldn't know where to go; I just couldn't. And then there's the building contractor who comes the very next morning; he rings at the door, just as you did. But you will let him in now; you'll tell him that you're my secretary; you'll tell him—But no, it's no use after all; I know well enough what he wants, and he knows how to get it; it wouldn't change anything. They took the lot for the road, for the school, and then they parceled out what was left; they built apartment buildings. But there's still this house; that's what they're after now, and they won't leave me a moment's rest until they've got it, and what for? To build more, still more. So I know that they'll come back in the night. They say it's the children from the juvenile home; that's what they say. But I know it's not true. It's them, all of them—the architect, the building contractor, the mayor and his deputies, all of them; they've been eyeing and coveting this property for such a long time now. They built the road right there in back; they thought I would leave on that account, but I closed the shutters; I don't open them anymore; I stay on the garden side . . . I'm so tired; sometimes I think I really should go, leave, let them have the house, so that they can finish their buildings, so that it'll all be over with. But I can't; I wouldn't know where to go, you see; I've lived in this house for so long, this is all I know now . . ."

That was how she spoke, with her soft voice that you could barely hear, and I watched the lovely light that changed imperceptibly in the large room filled with antique furniture because the sun was going down along its arched path in the empty sky. I thought of the old days, when I used to hide in the bushes of the garden, when the town was but a rumor, muffled by the trees at the foot of the hill. A number of times I was tempted to tell her what it was like in the old days, when I played in the garden, entering by the breach in the wall, and how the cats would scurry into the underbrush. I wanted to speak to her of the large, bright patch that would spring up between the palm trees suddenly, radiant, like a cloud, like a feather; I even started to tell her, "I remember, Ma'am; I . . ." But the words were left dangling, and the old lady looked at me calmly, with her clear eyes, and I don't know why, I didn't dare continue. Besides, my childhood memories seemed petty now that the city had eaten into Villa Aurora, for nothing could hide the wound, the pain, the anxiety that reigned here now. Then abruptly I knew that I couldn't stay in the house. The realization was like a shudder; it came over me all of a sudden. The destructive forces of the town—the cars, the buses, the trucks, the concrete mixers, the cranes, the pneumatic drills, the pulverizers—would all come here sooner or later; they would penetrate the sleeping garden and then the walls of the villa; they would shatter the windows, tear holes in the plaster ceilings, splinter the cane screens, crumble the yellow walls, the floorboards, the doorframes.

When I had grasped that, a feeling of emptiness crept

over me. The old lady had stopped talking. She was sitting there leaning slightly forward over the cup of tea growing cold, and she was watching the dwindling light through the window. Her lips quivered a bit, as though she were going to say something more. But she didn't speak again.

There was so much silence in her and here, in this dying villa. It had been ages since anyone had come. The contractors, the architects, even the deputy mayor, the one who had come with the ruling of expropriation in the interest of the general public before the school and the road had been built—no one came anymore; no one spoke anymore. So now it was the silence that was crushing the old house, killing it.

I don't know how I ended up leaving there. I think I must have slipped away like a coward, like a thief, just as the two young girls looking for an au pair room had fled before. The old lady was left alone in the middle of her big, forlorn house, alone in the large room with flaking plaster walls and amber-colored sunlight. I walked back down the streets, down the avenues, toward the bottom of the hill. The cars sped through the night, headlights bright, taillights fleeing. At the bottom, in the grooves of the boulevards, motors rumbled in unison, their clamor filled with menace and hate. Maybe this evening was the very last evening, when the young boys and girls from the juvenile home, their faces smeared with soot, would go into the sleep-filled garden with their knives and their chains. Or maybe on their motorcycles they would glide along the huge curve that crushed the old villa like the coil of a snake, and in passing, they would throw their empty Coca-Cola bottles on the flat roof, and maybe one of the bottles would be with burning gasoline . . . As I went into the crowd of cars and trucks between the high walls of the buildings, I thought I could hear, off in the distance, the wild cries of the city's thugs bringing down the roofs of Villa Aurora one after the other.

Translated by C. Dickson

When the Italians Came

François Maspero

LISE'S TRIP BEGAN on a rainy morning. The mother superior herself put her on the train, entrusting her to a family that filled an entire compartment. People were fighting to get in the doors, so she was passed up through a window. The German army had invaded the so-called Free Zone to counter the Allied landing in North Africa a few days before. People were snarling like whipped dogs.

The train mainly traveled on trunk lines. It crossed the Rhone during the day, and a chilled and hungry Lise had to change trains and wait on a station platform that the mistral scoured with gusts of ice crystals. Night fell

FRANÇOIS MASPERO (1932–) is an author and journalist and was a well-known publisher of leftist books in the 1970s. He has also translated books from English, Spanish, and Italian, including the works of Joseph Conrad and John Reed. His best-known books are *Le sourire du chat* (1985, tr. *Cat's Grin*), *Les passagers du Roissy-Express* (1990, tr. *Roissy Express*), and *Balkans-Transit* (1997). This excerpt from chapter 1 of *Le temps des Italiens* (1994) is set during the Italian army's invasion of Provence in 1942. Except for Toulon, the place names are made up.

at four o'clock, and it was in growing darkness that she reached Toulon, the great military port where the French navy had just scuttled its ships. That's why she always remembered the date of that trip. There she had to get to another station to catch the local that ran along the coast. It was raining as if the world were ending as she walked through a city of ghosts. The little train chugged off into the night. The lights in the wooden car were dim, travelers got off at deserted stations, Lise felt lost. When the train started up again, nothing else existed on Earth except its carcass clattering through the pitch darkness, punctuated by the panting of the locomotive. Rain lashed the windows, glowing cinders flew by. Lise was reduced to a frozen shiver. Finally, she saw a white glow on her right and pressed her face against the sticky window glass: the moon shone through the racing clouds. She glimpsed reflections: the sea. At the next stop, she could hear the rumble of waves in the intervals of silence between the gusts of wind, the hissing of steam, and the shouts of people in the darkness. The sea was close, so it had to be the Escarlène.

When she leaned out the window, a blast of moist air redolent of plants and the sea hit her face, and she spotted the conductor walking along the train with his rolling gait, his satchel casually slung over his shoulder. Lise had known him ever since she was a little girl. To her, he was the Train Man, the line's familiar genie. He always appeared out of the darkness the way he had this evening, sometimes coming into the car as they emerged from a tunnel, shuffling along on espadrilles even more worn than Lise's, wearing the uniform cap of the Compagnie des chemins de fer de Provence. A sagacious wisecracker, he would scrutinize tickets before punching them a seemingly random number of times, and occasionally consult thick wads of dog-eared lists and timetables. He was a past master at calculating schedules "given that we're running late," and since the train was always late, he was an oracle in great demand. A person out of the ordinary, in other words, whom Lise considered the equal in his own way of her grandfather Virgile. He shared the latter's accent, too, and not just the simple "Midi accent," but a whole skein of intimate and familiar nuances and intonations that told Lise that she was among her own people—here, and nowhere else. She never knew his name, they just called him "the conductor," and later, much later, he left her life with the shadow of the last train. On this night, his appearing was all it took for the world to regain its consistency. Lise called out to him, as she had often heard her grandmother do: Please Monsieur, ask the engineer to stop at the Pignerol level crossing before the La Rouquière station. The man raised his head to look at her, his small eyes wreathed in wrinkles, to say, This girl's crazy, it's been a long time since we stopped there; there hasn't been anybody at Pignerol since the beginning of the war. Well, *hardly* anybody. She wasn't actually going to Pignerol, she told him, but to the Dore house. The Dore house? He scratched his head. Like the ancient navigators, he probably kept in his head a current pilot's chart of the eighty kilometers of coastline he traveled along back and forth each day. It was his own personal nomenclature of places he would never visit, because he never left the stations and their snack bars, staying only long enough for a stop, an uncoupling, or an exchange of news between drinks. He must have known by heart a geography rooted in the regularly revisited faces of travelers who always got on and off at the same place, who walked down a road he could see snaking between vineyards and chestnut trees toward invisible hamlets, or who stepped out of some shack whose blank wall facing the tracks was all he knew, ignorant of its sunny side, with the shutters opened to cypress and orange trees. The Dore house? he repeated. So she was the Silvestrys' little girl? He caught himself and added, the *poor* little girl, to show that he knew all about it and wasn't mistaking her for anyone else. Suddenly aware of her status, Lise insisted: You see, I'm right, of course Pignerol is just a flag stop, but still, how about it? Well, the thing is, *they* are camped at the pass. He ran forward to the locomotive, Lisa could see him waving his arms, then he came back to tell her all right, but the engineer had confirmed it: *They* were camped there, and it wasn't very safe, but what the heck. I hope someone's meeting you at least, he added. He whistled, and the train lurched forward. A quarter of an hour later, it emerged from a tunnel and slowed in a clanking of colliding couplings. Lise jumped down to the spongy earth; the conductor had already whistled again.

When the train disappeared, the sound of the wind humming through the eucalyptus trees and the crash of waves rose to meet her. Bright lights appeared through the brush. The wind on her face brought the expected smells of the earth, the *maquis*, the flowers, and the sea, but mixed with clouds of acrid smoke. She looked at the lights: flames flared up unexpectedly, danced and twisted a while, then fell back into red incandescence. The night eliminated distances, and the wind created so many moving shadows that Lise couldn't tell if any of them were human. She heard a voice calling, and then her grandfather Virgile was next to her. She felt his hands on her shoulders and his mustache against her cheek. He lifted her up and she clung to him, her arms seeking his neck and her legs wrapped around his hips, but she couldn't find her familiar holds, and he soon put her down again. You've gotten too big, Lise, he said with a wheeze.

Let's go quickly, you're going to catch cold. Her grandfather was talking quietly, right into her ear, and she could smell that breath of his she also knew so well, of shag tobacco, wine, stale bread, and something hinting at the warmth of home. Leaning still closer, he too added: *They're* camped everywhere, as if that explained his haste.

This happened on November 30, 1942, around nine o'clock at night. At that point, all Lise had seen of the Italians were shadows.

Translated by William Rodarmor

The Ladle

Jean Failler

THE LITTLE PRIEST found himself out on Saint-Corentin Square, buffeted by a biting wind. He pulled his tricorn hat snugly down on his head before it could blow away, gathered the flapping folds of his cloak around him, and took a few uncertain steps. He had just emerged from the diocese office, where the bishop's secretary had summoned him on a matter of some importance.

His Excellency's secretary summoned minor parish priests only on matters of importance, in fact. Once again, it involved a shipwreck—what Bretons call a *bris*. A barge sailing from Bordeaux to Le Havre had been caught in a gale and blown ashore on the spit of the Tréguennec *palue*. While the surf was smashing the ship and scattering the wreckage across the wide beach, the news flashed from hut

JEAN FAILLER (1940–) is a very successful self-published writer of plays, short stories, and detective stories, nearly all set in different parts of his native Brittany. Several of his thirty-odd Mary Lester mysteries have been made into movies, but only *La cité des dogues* (1998) has been translated into English, as *Mayhem in Saint-Malo* (2003). This tale, which is set in the late eighteenth century, is from Failler's 1996 collection, *Le gros lot*.

to hut: "To the bris! To the bris!" The entire able-bodied population rushed out to scavenge this unexpected bounty. A bris at the beginning of winter—heaven was generous!

The mayor called up the Pont-l'Abbé police, but by the time the officers reached the site the next day, all that remained on the beach swept by a powerful nor'easter was a shattered, half-buried hull and a bare wooden frame. In the little Saint Vio church, five bodies lay stretched out on the cold tiles, completely naked.

The men of the palue had jumped into the freezing, waist-deep water to drag casks of wine onto the beach, where they tapped them and got roaring drunk. Like busy ants, the women and children gathered up everything they could.

So where were the barrels of wine destined for the Le Havre merchants? What about the crates of candles for the Rouen diocese? And the fine soap for the bourgeois of Paris, eh? Where were they?

The bishop's secretary bid the little priest answer, but he couldn't. The constabulary would search the houses of those wretches in Cap-Caval, warned the secretary, and woe to them if any evidence from the wreck turned up! They would go to prison, and certainly be damned to burn in hell forever!

The little priest weathered this jeremiad patiently. The police could go ahead and search those thatched huts where people and animals lived all jumbled together, but it would be a waste of time and effort. The booty had long since been hidden in invisible ravines, or in reed caches in treacherous swamps where no sensible person would dare to go.

The little priest knew his parishioners. They had been practicing the bris for a long time. For those impoverished people, a shipwreck was a gift from God. There had been other wrecks and other searches, and the policemen wouldn't find a single clue or shred of evidence, any more than they had in the past.

The dead would be laid to rest with all of the solemnity and reverence one could hope for, however. The entire parish would turn out for the funeral ceremony. Dressed in their Sunday best, people would piously sing the mass for the dead. (Some would be wearing the pants and pea coats of the unfortunate drowned men, who no longer needed them.) And, as usual, the little priest would give a severe and pointless sermon about other people's property, honesty, and all sorts of things that the palue people certainly didn't feel they were guilty of.

At the corner of the square, the post house stood glowing in the shadows. The little priest approached the tavern, which was Quimper-Corentin's finest, and gazed longingly through the heavy leaded windowpanes.

Of course, he didn't have the money to go warm his belly at the fire, sitting on one of those benches facing the big stone fireplace, and order a bowl of steaming broth. So he searched instead for some little corner out of the wind where he could wait for a cart that might take him back to his parish, where he could gnaw on the chunk of hard bread and three sour apples that were his only provisions.

"Hello, Father Floc'h!"

The little priest started, and turned around. Before him stood a priest of the handsomest sort, a sleek-faced cleric wearing a new cassock and a quilted overcoat. The little priest hid his piece of bread in his greenish sleeve, and awkwardly bobbed his head in greeting.

"I saw you at the chancery earlier," said the city priest in a well-modulated voice that probably sounded very impressive from the Saint-Corentin pulpit. "Did His Excellency call you in about that shipwreck business?"

It was more a statement than a question. The little priest again bobbed his head.

"What are you waiting here for?" asked the city priest.

"Nicolas Souron," said the little priest timidly. And since the man didn't seem to know this important figure in the Bigouden region, he added, "He's a pig merchant in Plonéour-Lanvern. He came in to sell some hogs to the city butchers. I'm waiting, and if he comes by, he'll give me a ride in his cart."

"What if he doesn't come by?"

"Then I'll walk home," said Floc'h with resignation.

"On foot? But your parish is at the ends of the earth!"

"Eight leagues," said the little priest with a thin smile. He glanced down at his much-mended boots. The prospect of hiking the eight leagues was nothing; his legs had certainly seen worse. But these were his only shoes, and they had to last him the whole winter.

"It will be night soon," added the city priest.

"I'm sure to find a shed along the way where I can sleep."

"Listen, Father Floc'h, I don't feel right letting you set out alone at this hour. Why don't you come to my place and have some dinner? You can sleep in a nice bed, and tomorrow you're sure to find a cart to take you to Pont-l'Abbé."

The gathering darkness was starting to hide the cathedral's massive towers, and the wind blew shrewdly. Hot soup, a bed . . . The little priest shivered with pleasure.

"Thank you," he said softly.

And he fell in behind the city priest.

The city priest lived in a handsome house on rue Verdelets, a narrow street behind the cathedral, and he made his guest welcome. Father Floc'h was abashed at the sight of the foyer, where he hung his cloak on a mahogany coat stand, the dining room with its polished oak floor, and the kitchen, which opened onto a small walled garden.

"I'll show you your room," said the city priest at the foot of the stairs. He added, as if in apology, "The house isn't very big. There are only three rooms upstairs. This one is yours."

He opened the door to a small room with whitewashed walls like a monk's cell. It was furnished with an iron bed with a crucifix hanging at its head. A pine wardrobe stood to the right of the bed, a small table with a pitcher and bowl to the left.

Again, he seemed to apologize. "It's pretty basic, isn't it?"

The little priest protested that it was better than what he had at home.

The city priest briefly opened another door off the hallway.

"This is my room," he said.

It was an exact copy of the first one. Then the priest closed the door, then, putting his fingers to his lips with a mysterious look, and opened a third one.

"This is my housekeeper's bedroom."

The little priest nearly whistled with admiration. The room was twice as big as the other two. It had a large cherry-wood bed, beautiful carpets, elegant wardrobes, comfortable chairs, and a handsome fireplace with a fire burning in it. In a word, everything in that room was so beautiful that the little Cap-Caval priest, who could hardly imagine that such luxury existed on this earth, might have briefly imagined himself at the gates of heaven.

Pleased with the impression he was making, the city priest gently closed the door, and they went down to the dining room.

The table was set with a white tablecloth, silver cutlery, and crystal glasses.

"You shouldn't have gone to such trouble," stammered the little priest.

The city priest smiled indulgently. Trouble? What was he talking about? He ate like this every day!

The little priest thought of his freezing rectory, his wobbly table of rough-hewn planks, his cracked bowl. Was a feeling of envy stirring in him? He quickly drove it away, because envy is a wicked sin.

"You can bring in the food, Henriette!" called the city priest. And Henriette entered bearing a steaming soup tureen as if it were the Blessed Sacrament. The handle of a silver ladle could be seen sticking above the rim.

The little priest was very hungry, and the tureen gave off a smell that would tempt a saint. But he couldn't take his eyes off the serving girl, the woman the city priest called Henriette. She was still young, with a smooth, gentle face—the face of a Madonna, thought the little priest.

But his gaze didn't stop at her face, may the Good Lord forgive him. Henriette had the full, generous body of a woman beneath a camisole stretched beyond imagining, and a gown that swayed voluptuously with her every step.

Resentfully, the little priest thought of his own house-keeper, Marie-Jeanne, with her grumpy expression, screechy voice, and skinny body.

Were thoughts of lust rising within him? He quickly drove them away, because lust is a great sin.

The city priest served him some stew. The little priest first sniffed it, then tasted it with delight. He couldn't remember ever eating such a delicious pot-au-feu, unless it was when the manor lord's daughter got married. He crossed himself, thanking God for having put this hospitable city priest on his path. The latter poured him a glass of red wine from a gleaming ruby carafe. Lord, how good it was!

For a moment, and only for a moment, Father Floc'h thought of the bad cider that he usually drank. Meanwhile, the city priest was talking. He had ideas about everything, this priest, on what should be done to the wreckers who were bringing dishonor to our coasts. Didn't they hang lanterns from their cows' horns, to lure ships onto the rocks? The city priest came from a family of ship owners, and these bandits' actions were ruining them.

Between two bites of food and two sips of wine, the little priest raised his hand, but it wasn't clear if it was to agree or to weakly protest. Ah, if this was the wine his flock had appropriated, he'd happily accept a cask of it.

The dining room was lit as bright as day by four chandeliers with five candles each. Ah, if these were the candles his parishioners had seized, a few dozen would be welcome for the parish and the church.

The splendid silver ladle glittered when the city priest gave him a third helping, which he accepted without objection.

The little priest wiped his mouth with a white napkin that smelled freshly laundered. Ah, if this was the soap that the people of the palue had salvaged from the sea, they should keep a crate of it for him, by heaven! His clothes would smell fresh, for once!

Henriette reappeared, majestically carrying a platter of meat and vegetables. The little priest's eyes gleamed with covetousness. Again, he crossed himself and thanked heaven for his good fortune. He was a good man, thankful for what he was given, and had no bitterness. He didn't think that with a little luck he too might have been born to a family of ship owners and not to a poor laborer, and that he could be a cathedral rector in the rich city of Quimper instead of a country priest in the barren palue of Cap-Caval.

Meanwhile, the city priest was still discoursing on honesty, virtue, heaven, and hell.

The little priest listened to him absently, while thinking that it's easy to be virtuous when your feet are warm and your stomach is full.

Henriette came to clear the table. The good food, the wine, the warmth from the fireplace, and the glow of the candles had all loosened the little priest's tongue.

He thanked his host and complimented the cook, who gave him a thin smile as she left. When the two men were alone, the little priest repeated his compliment.

"You're a lucky man, Father! Your housekeeper is a real gem. I've never eaten such a good pot-au-feu in my life!"

The city priest acted modest. His eyes said: This is what I eat every day. You should see the days when I have company!

"And what a beautiful woman!" added the little priest.

He was just talking, without any ill intention, but the city priest's head snapped up.

The little priest, who hadn't noticed, continued: "She could pose—"

"Father Floc'h!" thundered the city priest.

The little priest started, and looked up in surprise. Had he said something inappropriate? He finished the sentence in a shaky voice, while giving his host a worried glance: "—she could pose for a statue of the Virgin Mary!"

The city priest sighed and relaxed.

"For a moment there, I was afraid that you were going to make a joke in bad taste about my housekeeper's person."

"Me?" exclaimed the little priest in astonishment. "Heaven forbid, Father!" and he crossed himself.

The city priest crossed himself in turn and said, "Forgive me, Father Floc'h, if I ascribed evil thoughts to you. But you see," he crossed himself again, "our Lord has said that we must not only preach, but also set an example, keep our souls pure and our minds free of thoughts of debauchery and fornication."

He pursued this line of thinking for a good ten minutes, as if he were preaching from the pulpit. The sermon was so beautiful that the little priest listened open-mouthed, and when it was over, had to restrain himself from applaud-

ing. He merely crossed himself and said, "Amen." Then
they each went upstairs to his room.

The next day, after an excellent night's sleep, the little
priest got a ride on a cart that was delivering nails to the
Plomeur blacksmith.

Three days later, Henriette went to find the city priest.

"Ah, Father, I'm in a fix! I can't find the silver soup
ladle!"

"What?" cried the city priest. "You've lost my beautiful
ladle?"

"I haven't lost anything," she snapped. "I just haven't
seen it since . . . since I made that pot-au-feu!"

"But how could it be that—"

"It's that you bring anyone at all home with you!"

"Do you mean to say—"

"I mean to say that the ladle disappeared after the visit
by that little priest, you know, the one from Cap-Caval.
The one who threw himself on the food as if he were
starving!"

The city priest put on in his most severe expression.

"Come now, my girl—a little Christian charity! What
makes you say that poor man stole my ladle?"

Henriette put her fists on the very hips that the little
priest had so admired. "Who else could it be?" she asked
vehemently. "No one has come to the house since his
visit!"

The city priest was very troubled. Of course poor Father
Floc'h could have been the one to take the precious ladle.
But on the other hand, nothing proved it. And if he was
innocent, accusing him would be a serious matter.

He spent a long time meditating, then praying over the matter. He called on Santig-Du, Brittany's patron saint of lost objects, but in vain. The ladle was nowhere to be found.

He decided to explain his problem to a Jesuit, who gave him some sound advice.

That evening, the city priest carefully trimmed a handsome goose feather and set a spotless sheet of paper on his lectern. After a moment's final thought, he firmly dipped his quill in the horn inkwell and wrote:

To the Reverend Pierre-Marie Floc'h,
Cap-Caval.
Greetings Father,

I have been dealing with a strange mystery since the day of your visit to my house on rue Verdelets.

You may find it hard to believe, but my ladle has disappeared. I'm sure you remember it. It was the handsome silver ladle that my housekeeper Henriette used to serve us her pot-au-feu.

My faithful servant has been angry ever since, and the quality of her cooking has suffered. You can imagine how upset I am! That ladle came down to me from my mother, and quite aside from its worth, which is considerable, it has great sentimental value.

Since you are the only person to have visited us since its disappearance, Henriette has come to an unpleasant conclusion.

For myself, I am not saying that you borrowed the ladle for some noble purpose. I am definitely not saying that.

However, if you could help us to clear up this mystery, I would be infinitely grateful.

With my most sincere Catholic and Apostolic wishes,
Jean Rousseau,
Rector of the Cathedral
Quimper–Corentin

The little priest received the missive in his chilly rectory. When he read it, a slight smile lit up his thin face. He sat down at his wobbly table and wrote:

To the Reverend Jean Rousseau
Rector of the Cathedral
Quimper–Corentin.
Greetings Father,
I haven't thanked you enough for your warm welcome. It was truly wonderful, and I will long remember it.
You ask me for news of that beautiful ladle you received from madame your mother. Let me say that I am surprised and alarmed by how many sleepless nights your ecclesiastical devotion in the great city of Quimper-Corentin must be costing you.
You have apparently spent nearly a week in service to His Excellency the bishop, and haven't had the leisure of sleeping in your own bed. If you had, you would have not failed to find your ladle there, nice and warm under the quilt.
I hope I have been of assistance to you. Please accept my most sincere Catholic, Apostolic, and Roman wishes.
Pierre–Marie Floc'h
Beuzec Cap–Caval Parish

Translated by William Rodarmor

A Frozen Woman

Annie Ernaux

FRAGILE AND VAPORISH WOMEN, spirits with gentle hands, good fairies of the home who silently create beauty and order, mute, submissive women—search as I may, I cannot find many of them in the landscape of my childhood. Not even in the next-best model, less elegant, more frumpy, the ones who work miracles with leftovers, scrub the sink until you can see your face in it, and take up their posts outside the school gates fifteen minutes before the last bell rings, all their housework done. Perfectly organized unto death. The women in my life all had loud voices, untidy bodies that were too fat or too flat, sand-papery fingers, faces without a trace of makeup or else

---

ANNIE ERNAUX (1940–) has made her reputation as a writer of a series of relentlessly honest autobiographical novels. They describe her childhood in Yvetot, Normandy (*La honte*, 1997, tr. *Shame*), her adolescence (*Ce qu'ils disent ou rien*, 1977), her marriage (*La femme gelée*, 1981, tr. *A Frozen Woman*), her abortion (*L'événement*, 2000, tr. *Happening*), and her mother's death (*Une femme*, 1989, tr. *A Woman's Story*). This excerpt is from the start of Linda Coverdale's 1996 translation of *A Frozen Woman*.

---

slathered in it, with big blotches of color on the cheeks and lips. Their cooking skills did not go much beyond stewed rabbit and rice pudding, they had no idea dust was supposed to be removed on a daily basis, they worked or had worked on farms, in factories, in small businesses open all day long. There were the old ladies we visited on Sunday afternoons, with their boudoirs and the bottle of eau-de-vie to sweeten their coffee, wizened women all in black whose skirts smelled of butter going rancid in the pantry. No connection with those sugary grandmas in story books who wear their snow-white hair in a neat bun and coo over their grandchildren while they read them fairy tales. My old ladies, my granny and my great-aunts, they weren't nearly that chummy and didn't like it when you jumped all over them—they'd lost the habit. A peck on the cheek was all, at the beginning and end of the visit, so after the inevitable "You've gone and grown some more!" and "Still studying hard in school?" they really had nothing more to say to me, too busy talking with my parents in patois about the high cost of living, the rent, the lack of living space, the neighbors; they'd look over at me every once in a while, laughing. On Sundays in the summertime, we visited Aunt Caroline, hiking along bumpy roads that turned into quagmires at the slightest shower, bound for the back of beyond—two or three farms and their pastures lying out on a plain. Caroline was never home, so after a perfunctory knock on the door, we'd check with the neighbors and eventually find her tying up bunches of onions or helping out with a calving. She'd come home, poke at the fire in her wood stove, break up some kindling, and fix us a light meal of soft-boiled eggs, bread and butter, and parsnip wine. A real wonder, that woman. "You're still bursting with health, Caroline! Aren't you bored out here?" She thought that was funny. "What do you mean," she'd protest, "there's always things needing doing." "Ever get scared, you know, all alone?" That really surprised her, put a twinkle in her eye. "What could anyone get up to with me, at my age?" I didn't listen much, and slipping past the blind wall of the house, edged with nettles taller than I was, I'd go off to the pond to pick through the broken plates and tin cans my auntie dumped down there, all rusty and full of water teeming with bugs. Caroline would walk a little way along with us when we left, a good kilometer or so in nice weather. Then our bikes would leave her behind, a tiny dot in the fields of colza. I knew that this eighty-year-old woman, swathed in blouses and skirts even in the worst of the dog days, needed neither pity nor protection. No more than did Aunt Elise, swimming in her own lard but full of bounce, and a lousy housekeeper: when I crawled around under her bed my dress picked up dust pom-poms, and I'd inspect the dried crud on my spoon for a moment before daring to plunge it through the wrinkled skin of my poached pear. "What's the matter with you, you're not eating?" she'd ask, and her puzzlement would explode into a huge guffaw. "That itty-bitty pear isn't going to plug up your fanny-hole!" Then there was my grandmother, who lived in a crummy prefab between the railway and the lumberyard in the neighborhood called la Gaieté. Whenever we arrived, she would be gathering greens for the rabbits or doing some mending or washing, which irritated my mother. "Why can't you take it easy, at your age?" Reproaches like that exasperated my grandmother, who only a few years earlier had been hauling herself up to the railroad tracks by gripping clumps of grass, so that she could sell apples and cider to the American soldiers after the Normandy invasion. She'd grumble a bit, then bring in the pot of boiling hot coffee threaded with white foam and pour a drop of eau-de-vie on the sugar stuck to the bottom of the cups; everyone would swirl the brandy gently around. They'd talk, nattering on about the neighbors, a landlord who wouldn't make repairs, and I'd be a touch bored, as there was nothing to explore in that little house without a proper yard, and almost nothing to eat. My grandmother would slurp greedily at the dregs in her cup. Her high cheekbones were as shiny as the yellow boxwood egg she used to darn socks. Sometimes, when she thought she was alone out in her scrap of a garden, she peed standing up, spreading her legs beneath her long black skirt. And yet, she had come in first in the canton on the exam for the primary school certificate, so she could have been a teacher, but my great-grandmother had said not on your life, she's my eldest girl and I need her at home to raise the other five. A story told a hundred times, why her life hadn't come up roses. Once she'd been like me, running around, going to school, with no idea what was coming, and then disaster struck: with five youngsters to hold her back, she was finished. What I didn't understand was why she later had six of her own, without any dependents' allowances, either. You didn't need a map to figure out early on that kids—chicks, everyone I knew used to call them—put you truly in the hole, just buried you alive. And at the same time it seemed irresponsible, careless, the sort of thing you'd expect from poor people who had no common sense. Those large families I saw all around me meant swarms of runny-nosed brats, women pushing baby carriages and staggering along with bags of groceries, and constant griping at the end of every month. Granny had fallen into the trap but you couldn't blame her, back then it was normal to have six, ten children; we've come a long way since. My aunts and uncles were so fed up with big families that my cousins are all only children. I'm an only child, too, and an afterthought as well—that's what they call children born late in life, when a couple who hadn't wanted any (or any more) change their minds. I was their one and only, period. I was convinced I was really lucky.

The sole exception was Aunt Solange, poor Solange with that brood of hers, my mother always said. She lived in la Gaieté, too, and we often went there on Sundays. The neighborhood was like a vast playground where you could do anything you wanted. In the summer, I'd join my seven cousins and their friends, shrieking on the seesaws we made from planks stacked next to the lumberyard. In the winter we played tag in the one big bedroom crammed with beds. I adored all this warmth and uproar, almost enough to want to live there, but my Aunt Solange frightened me. She was old before her time, always puttering in her kitchen, her mouth twitching uncontrollably. Once she spent months laid up in bed when her uterus decided to prolapse on her. Then there were the times when she would get this vacant look in her eyes; she'd open a window, close it, move the chairs around, and bang, she'd start screaming that she was going to take the children and leave, that she had always been unhappy, while my uncle just sat calmly at the table, glass in hand, not saying a word or else sneering, "You wouldn't have any idea where to go, you idiot." She'd rush weeping out into the courtyard, threatening to throw herself into the cistern, but her children or the neighbors would grab her first. As for us, we'd head tactfully for the door as soon as the shouting started. Looking back, I would see the youngest girl crying openmouthed, her teary face pressed against the windowpane.

I don't know if my other aunts were happy, but they didn't have that beaten-down air Solange had, and they didn't let anyone slap them around. With their red cheeks and lips, they were always in a fever of activity, always in a hurry, with barely a moment to stop on the sidewalk, clutching their grocery bags as they leaned down to give me a little air kiss and rumble, "What have you been up to, my girl?" No fond displays of affection, either, none of those puckered-up mouths or cajoling looks people use to talk to children. These women were a bit stiff, abrupt, with tempers that exploded in swear words. At the end of family dinners, at First Communions, they would laugh until they cried, burying their faces in their napkins. My Aunt Madeleine would practically split her face in half, she'd laugh so hard. I don't remember ever seeing a single one of them knitting or patiently stirring a sauce; they'd serve cold cuts and other *charcuterie*, then produce from the pantry a pyramid of white paper stained with pastry cream. They couldn't have cared less about dusting and cleaning, although they made the ritual apologies, "Please, just pay no attention to the mess." Not domestic, these women, nothing but outdoor types, used to working like men ever since they were twelve years old, and not even somewhere clean, like a textile mill, but in a rope factory or cannery. I liked to listen to them, ask them questions about the whistle, the coveralls they had to wear, the fore-woman, the times when they'd all be laughing together in the same room, and it seemed to me that they were going to school, too, only they didn't get homework or detention. At first, before I began to admire teachers, those awesome and superior beings, before I learned that watching jars fill up with pickles is not a great profession, I thought what my aunties did was a fine way to earn a living.

Translated by Linda Coverdale

Just Like an Actress
Eric Holder

IF YOU WANT TO BUY a baguette or a roll—a *chocolatine*, as they call them in the Landes—the place to go is over toward Luglon, where the low houses with their roofs like women's wide-brimmed gardening hats look anxious about being squeezed together.

Sometimes, parked on the pavement out front, there's a car from somewhere else, its license plate with some code other than the local one: 40. They're tourists on their way to Mimizan. Or else they've come to visit the Parc régional, which you reach from the railway station in the town; it's the train's only stop. When men step into the bakery, they take off their sunglasses. That's because it's dark inside, and because she's beautiful.

ERIC HOLDER (1960–) was born in Lille, spent his youth in Provence, and now lives in Médoc, north of Bordeaux. His many novels include *Bruits de coeurs* (1994), *Mademoiselle Chambon* (1996), and *Les sentiers délicats* (2005), and often deal with the peregrinations of the heart. This story appears in *En compagnie des femmes* (1996). It is set in the Landes, south of Bordeaux, and uses two local terms: an *airial* is an open grassy space surrounded by oaks; *fougasse* is a flat bread, like focaccia.

Impossibly beautiful, with her luxuriant hair, enormous eyes, lips both finely drawn and sensuously full. She recognizes the surprised expression on all their faces as they push the door open, that look that says, What in God's name is she doing here? She recognizes it, but she hasn't gotten used to it. She still trembles slightly as she hands them their change. She doesn't look at the customers directly and especially not at their cars, either, as they drive off toward the beaches and the hotels with swimming pools.

Once, a young man who was less shy than the others— from Paris, probably—took her hand and said, "Haven't we met somewhere before?" She pulled her hand away and shrugged slightly. Where could anyone have met her except at the bakery?

Farther out, the houses no longer keep their distance from one another, the way Landes people famously do. But they're readying themselves for isolation. Some still try to show a touch of humanity with their fences, their tidy little gardens, their newly painted gates. Then there's a field, like a breathing space needed before you're finally plunged into the forestry plantation, that desert of pine trees in long rows, broken only by the occasional broom bush. Sometimes a dirt road leads through a gap in the wall of trees to a farm where there are dogs.

She looks just like an actress. It was her father who said it first. When she was, what, thirteen? Fourteen? It was late in the afternoon. He had just woken from a nap and was drinking his coffee at the table upstairs where she was doing her homework. It was one of those moments of silence when time seems to stand still, the last orange rays of the sun lingering on the ceiling moldings. He wasn't thinking about his batches of bread, his orders, his Sunday specialty of stuffed *fougasse*. He was looking at his daughter, taking in the thick braid of hair, the huge eyes, and the cherry-colored mouth, and was stunned. "You look just like an actress." The statement hung in the air between them, floating in the room, cradled like a jewel in the silence. She looked up and was struck by the expression on her father's face. An expression that was, well, respectful.

Ever since then, when she thinks of her father or hears him working at the oven at night, that's how she pictures him, looking at her from behind his bowl of coffee, upstairs, that time when on his face, still puffy with sleep, she read fear mixed with astonishment.

Not long after that, she found her mother's magazines in the attic. Old issues of *Cinémonde*, *Noir et Blanc*, and *Intimité*. She realized that she didn't look like anyone from around here, but that she did somewhat resemble Tilda Thamar, "the orchid girl" in the retouched photos. Antonella Lualdi kisses Franco Interlenghi. Barbara Laage to be Henri Vidal's new costar.

She took the magazines downstairs to her room, where they lie in a pile under her bed. She must prefer them to the ones you can buy at the gas station: *Première*, or *Studio*. She relates best to the kind of caption under the photos that say: "A captivating Kitty de Hoyos reveals all in *Unfaithful Wives*. Her performance causes a stir."

For much the same reason, she hardly ever goes to the movies anymore, though there's a movie theater in the town. It's squeezed between the *airial*, the school, and the community center at the far side of the square, where lounging yellow dogs add a South American touch. Sometimes the posters arrive late, and the movie titles are listed in green felt marker instead. She's tempted, then disappointed. She wants languorous beauties in evening gowns; she gets bloody thrillers. Around her the empty seats spread out in the shape of a cross. Three rows in front, the boys all turn around and blush.

Every couple of days, Claude comes to see her. They met at primary school. He's already quite stocky, plays rugby, is from Luglon. These days he's a salesman, wines and spirits. He himself doesn't drink.

He pops in when they're not busy, when she can't bear it anymore, staring out at the house across the road that hasn't changed since the day she was born. He tells her funny stories, shares news about Bordeaux, which he often visits. And sometimes he doesn't talk, just stares out in the same direction she does, through the window. He isn't married. He's waiting.

On Mondays in the summertime, she takes the little train to Marquèze, in the Parc régional, where a historic "neighborhood" has been preserved, a farm from the time of the Grande-Lande. She wears sunglasses and a dress that shows off her figure. High-heeled shoes make her as tall and slender as a model.

She shivers with anticipation each time she gets off the train. Here are the sheep grazing in the meadow, the fields of millet and rye, the landowner's and the tenant's houses, the sheepfold. She's convinced they'll be scouting locations here someday. An assistant director with a camera will have found the best spot to film the sweeping historical epic. She'll let him approach her. "Excuse me, miss, would you mind if I took your photo, while I'm at it? Okay, got it. Thank you."

Later, in Paris: "Shit, man! Are you worth what we pay you, or what? She's a local, you said? You gotta be kidding. Know what you're gonna do? Get back in your car right now. You go back and you leave no stone unturned until you find her again."

The park guide notices that she's a regular, so he always adds some little extra detail to his commentary, just for her. He's a great fan of the Grande-Lande, and thinks a little detail will stimulate her interest in history. It's so rare for the locals to . . .

She realizes what he's doing. She pretends to understand, but all the while she's looking for the man among all these tourists who will step out of the group, some day.

Sometimes there's a clearing in the middle of the trees—a couple of hectares, maybe more—that the tractors and regional preserves have missed. It's a forgotten piece of the Landes, a patch that has never been taken over. You can walk there between the silvery puddles. In some of the bigger ones, grasses grow; logs lie slowly bleaching; bulrushes can be seen. It could be the Camargue, except that when you look up your view is blocked by the pine trees. And the sky, stretching right across the horizon, with that intensely solitary sun, its rays, like frost on your hands, freezing or burning, who can tell. It's not harsh, or grim. Just wild and terrifying.

She goes to Bordeaux, now. She even belongs to an

association that hosts visitors from a sister city, she shows them around the monuments. On Sundays, Claude takes their older child to the rugby games. He thinks their little girl, who's five, takes after her mother. The same already luxuriant hair, the same eyes, like the ones the Arab poet described so well when he wrote that those were the eyes God had in mind when he first created eyes. Holding her hand, he doesn't know which feeling is stronger, embarrassment or pride. He often says "my daughter," stressing the *my*. They sell a few groceries at the bakery now. They're thinking of adding a snack bar. Just a little one, that would be great.

Translated by Jean Anderson

Junior
Anna Gavalda

HIS NAME IS ALEXANDRE DEVERMONT. He's a young man, all pink and blond.

Raised in a vacuum. Nothing but baby wipes and anticavity toothpaste, with lisle shirts and a dimple in his chin. Cute. Clean. A little suckling piglet.

He'll be twenty soon, that depressing age when you think everything is possible. So many possibilities, and so many illusions. So many hard knocks to come, too.

But not for this pink young man. Life has never treated him badly. No one's ever pulled his ears hard enough to really hurt. He's a good boy.

ANNA GAVALDA (1970–) is a journalist and award-winning novelist whose debut short-story collection, *Je voudrais que quelqu'un m'attende quelque part* (1999, tr. *I Wish Someone Were Waiting for Me Somewhere*), sold more than three-quarters of a million copies in France. Her novels include *Je l'aimais* (2002, tr. *Someone I Loved*), *35 kilos d'espoir* (2002, tr. *95 Pounds of Hope*), *Ensemble c'est tout* (2005, tr. *Hunting and Gathering*), and *La consolante* (2008).

His maman puts on airs. She says, "Hello, this is Eliza-beth De-vermont," pronouncing the "de" separately, as if she still hoped to fool people. No such luck. There are a lot of things you can buy nowadays, but the little "de" that says you're nobility isn't one of them.

You can't just go shopping for that kind of bloodline. It's like with Obélix, you had to have fallen into the magic potion cauldron when you were little. Which doesn't stop maman from wearing a signet ring with a coat of arms.

What kind of arms? I wonder. A jumbled crown and fleurs-de-lys on a shield. The French butchers and caterers trade association uses the same coat of arms on its letter-head stationery, but she doesn't know that. Just as well.

His papa joined the family business, Meubles Rofitex, a manufacturing company. It makes white fiberglass lawn furniture.

Guaranteed not to yellow for ten years, in any climate.

Of course, fiberglass makes you think of picnics in trailer-trash campgrounds. Teak would be more elegant, you could craft classic benches that slowly take on a lovely patina and accumulate lichens under the centuries-old oak tree your great-grandfather planted in the middle of the estate. But hey, you have to take what's left to you, right?

Speaking of furniture, I was exaggerating a little be-fore when I said that life had never put Junior though the wringer. It did once, actually. One day when he was danc-ing with a young girl from a good family, a girl as slim and lean as a purebred English setter, he got the shock of his young life.

It happened during one of those little society parties that the mothers throw at huge expense to keep their offspring from straying and laying their heads on the breasts of some dusky girl who smells of exotic spices and danger.

Anyway, there was Alexandre with his wing collar shirt and his sweaty palms, dancing with this girl and being careful to keep his fly from brushing against her belly. He was trying to swing his hips a little, keeping time with the taps on his Westons. You know, like relaxed and all. Like young.

Then the girl asked him, "What does your father do?" (That's a question girls ask at these sorts of get-togethers.)

Twirling her around, he answered mock-absentmindedly, "He's the CEO of Rofitex. Dunno if you know the company. Two hundred employ—"

She didn't give him time to finish. She abruptly stopped dancing, her English setter eyes wide.

"Wait a minute—Rofitex? You mean . . . You mean Rofitex condoms?"

Man, it was too much!

"No, lawn furniture," he sputtered, completely at a loss. What a birdbrain this girl was! What a total birdbrain! Fortunately the music ended then, and Alexandre fled to the buffet to drink a little champagne and get something to eat. He really couldn't believe it.

Turned out the girl wasn't even one of the gang, she'd just crashed the party.

Twenty years old. My God.

Young Devermont had to take the *baccalauréat* exam twice before passing, but he had no problem with his driver's license. He passed the test the first time out, and had just gotten his license.

Not like his brother, who'd needed three tries.

So, everybody was in a good mood at dinner. The licence wasn't quite a done deal yet because the local driving examiner was a real asshole. A drunk, too. We're in the country here.

Like his brother and his cousins before him, Alexandre learned to drive during summer vacation at his grandmother's place, because the fees are cheaper in the provinces than in Paris. There's almost a thousand-franc difference in the price of a driving-school course.

Anyway, the drunk was still reasonably sober, and he signed the pink form without being snotty about it.

Alexandre was allowed to use his mother's Golf when she didn't need it, otherwise he could take the old Peugeot 104 in the shed. Like the others.

The 104 was still in good shape, but it smelled of chicken shit.

Summer vacation was nearly over. It would soon be time to go back to Paris and the big apartment on avenue Mozart, and start the private business school on avenue de Saxe. A school whose diploma wasn't yet recognized by the state, but which had a complicated name with lots of initials—something like SWSA (Scions with Supercilious Attitudes), MOTIT (Masters of the Universe in Training), or WAOB (Widows and Orphans Beware).

Our little piglet has certainly changed during the summer months. He's loosened up some, and has even started smoking.

Marlboro Lights.

It's because of his new friend. He now pals around with Franck Mingeaut, the son of a big local farmer. A real piece of work, that Franck: loud, lively, and loaded. Politely says hello to Alexandre's grandmother while leering at his pretty cousins. Tsk-tsk . . .

Knowing Junior makes Franck Mingeaut happy. Thanks to Alex, Franck has access to society, goes to parties where the girls are slender and attractive, and drinks the family champagne instead of Valstar beer. Instinctively, he knows that's the way to set himself up in life. Smoking in the back rooms of cafés, pawing hairy maids, shooting pool, and going to county fairs is all very well for a while, but investing an evening with So-and-So's daughter at Chateau So-and-So is energy well spent.

Junior is happy with his nouveau riche pal, too. Thanks to Franck, Alex gets to career around gravel courtyards in a sports car, roar down Touraine's departmental highways giving the finger to peasants to make them get their vans out of his way, and to hell with his father. He's undone another shirt button, and has even taken to wearing his baptismal medal on a slender chain around his neck—a young tough with a soft side. Girls love that.

This evening is *the* party of the summer. Count and Countess de LaRochepoobah are throwing an open house for Eléonore, their youngest. The upper crust from Mayenne to deepest Berry will be there, the whole damn Bottin Mondain social register, with more virgin heiresses than you can shake a stick at.

And money. Not the clink of money, but the smell of money. Plunging necklines, creamy skin, pearl necklaces, ultralight cigarettes, and giggly laughter. For Franck of the Chunky Bracelet and Alexandre of the Slender Chain, this is the big night.

No way they're going to miss it.

To the count and countess, a rich farmer will always be a peasant, and a well-brought-up businessman will always be a shop clerk. All the more reason to drink their champagne and screw their daughters in the bushes. Besides, not all those maidens are cold. They're direct descendants of Godfrey of Bouillon, and some of them don't mind pushing the last Crusade a little farther.

Franck doesn't have an invitation, but Alexandre knows the guy who'll be at the front door, no problem, you slip him a hundred francs and he'll let you in. If you like, he'll even announce you, the way they do at cotillions.

The car's the big problem. A car matters, if you want to hook up with girls who don't want to get their asses all scratched up in the bushes.

A cutie who doesn't want to leave the party too early ditches her papa and has to find an escort to take her home later. So if you're a boy and you don't have a car in an area where people live miles from each other, you're either screwed or you're a virgin.

And there, the situation is critical. Franck's chick magnet is in the shop for a tune-up, and Alexandre doesn't have his mother's Golf: she's driven it to Paris.

What's left? The sky-blue 104 with chicken shit on the seats and along the doors. There's even straw on the floorboards and a sticker on the windshield that reads "Hunting is natural." Lord, what a losermobile.

"What about your old man? Where is he?"

"He's traveling."

"What about his car?"

"It's here. Why do you ask?"

"Why's it here?"

"Because Jean-Raymond is supposed to clean it inside and out."

(Jean-Raymond is the handyman.)

"Then it's perfect! We just borrow his ride for the evening, bring it back, slam-bam-thank-you-ma'am, and nobody's the wiser."

"Uh-uh, Frank. No can do. Can't do that."

"Why not?"

"Listen, if anything happened, I'd get killed. Uh-uh, no can do."

"What the hell do you think could happen, numb-nuts? What d'you think could happen, huh?"

"Uh-uh."

"Quit giving me that goddamned 'Uh-uh!' Where's that at, anyway? It's fifteen kilometers there and fifteen back. The road's straight as an arrow and there won't be a soul out at that time of night. So tell me, what's the problem?"

"If there's the slightest hitch . . ."

"What kind of hitch, huh? What kind of fucking hitch? I've had my license for three years now and I've never had a single problem, you hear me? Not one," says Franck, flicking his thumb across an eyetooth.

"Uh-uh, no way. Not my dad's Jaguar."

"I can't believe what a jerk you're being! I can't believe it!"

". . ."

"So what do we do? Go to La Roche-my-nuts in that rolling henhouse of yours?"

"Well, yeah."

"But aren't we supposed to bring your cousin and then pick up her girlfriend at Saint-Chinan?"

"Well, yeah."

"And you think they're going to plunk their little butts down on seats covered with chicken shit?"

"Well, no."

"Well, there you go! We borrow your dad's car, we take a little spin, and in a few hours we put it back where we took it. That's all there is to it."

"Uh-uh, not the Jaguar." A pause. "Not the Jag."

"Then I'll find someone else to take me. You really are an asshole. This is the party of the summer, and you want us to show up in your cattle truck? No fucking way. Does it even run?"

"Sure it runs."

"Son of a bitch, I can't believe this."

He pulls on the skin of his cheeks.

"Anyway, you can't get into the party without me."

"Yeah, well, I don't know which is worse, not going or going in that garbage can of yours. Hey, see that there isn't still a chicken in there, okay?"

On the road home. Five o'clock in the morning. Two gray, tired boys who smell of cigarettes and sweat, but not of fornication (good party, no score, it happens).

Two silent boys on the Indre-et-Loire D49 highway between Bonneuil and Cissé-le-Duc.

"So ya see . . . We din' break it, did we? . . . You din'

have to run your damn 'Uh-uh' number on me. Big Raymond can polish daddy's car tomorrow."

"Hmpf! For all the good it did us, we could have taken the other one."

"True, no luck in that department . . ."

Franck squeezes his crotch.

"Din' make a lot of friends tonight, did ya, huh? . . . Still, I made a date to play tennis tomorrow with a blonde with big tits."

"Which one?"

"You know, the one who—"

Franck never finished that sentence because a wild pig—a boar weighing at least a hundred and fifty kilos—chose just that moment to cross the road without looking right or left, the idiot.

A pig in a hurry, probably rushing home from a party and afraid that his parents would chew him out.

First they heard the screech of tires, then a huge *bonk!* in front.

"Oh, shit," said Alexandre Devermont.

They stopped, opened the doors, and went to see. The pig was stone dead and so was the right front of the car: no bumper, no radiator, no headlights, no fender. Even the little Jaguar hood ornament had taken a hit.

"Oh, shit," Alexandre Devermont said again.

He was too drunk and too tired to say anything else. And yet at that precise moment, he was already aware— *clearly* aware—of the enormous shit storm that was gathering around him.

Franck kicked the dead pig in the gut and said, "Well,

we aren't gonna leave it here. Let's bring it home, at least. We'll barbecue it."

Alexandre started to laugh quietly.

"Yeah, roast boar's pretty good."

It wasn't funny at all—in fact, the situation was pretty serious—but the two started laughing hysterically. Probably because they were tired and nervous.

"You'll see, your mom'll be happy."

"Fer sure, she'll be pleased as hell!"

The two idiots laughed so hard their sides ached.

"So well . . . We gonna stick it in the trunk?"

"Yeah."

"Shit!"

"What now?"

"Trunk's full of stuff."

"Huh?"

"It's full, I'm telling ya. There's your dad's golf bag and a bunch of cases of wine in there."

"Oh, shit."

"What d'we do?"

"We'll stick it in the back, on the floor."

"Think so?"

"Yeah, just a sec. I'll put something down to protect the seats. Look in the back of the trunk for a car rug."

"A what?"

"A car rug."

"Wha's that?"

"That thing with the green and blue squares there, all the way in the back."

"Ah, a blanket! One of those Paris things."

"Whatever. C'mon, hurry."

"Wait, I'll help you. No point in messing up the leather seats, too."

"You're right."

"Son of a bitch, it's heavy!"

"No shit."

"Stinks, too."

"Hey, Alex, we're in the country."

"Screw the country."

They got back into the car and started it with no trouble. The motor was apparently all right. That was something, anyway.

But a few kilometers farther, they got the scare of their lives. It started with some noises and grunting behind them.

"Son of a bitch!" said Franck. "That fucker isn't dead!"

Alexandre didn't answer. It was really all too much.

The pig stood up and began turning around.

Franck slammed on the brakes and screamed, "Let's get the hell out of here!"

He was white as a sheet.

The doors slammed and they got away from the car. Inside, it was total shit.

Total. Shit.

The cream-colored leather bucket seats: smashed. The steering wheel: smashed. The burr elm gearshift: smashed. The headrests: smashed. The car's whole interior: smashed, smashed, smashed.

Devermont Junior: crushed.

The animal's eyes were bulging, and white foam slathered his long, curved tusks. A horrible sight.

They decided to open the car door and use it as a shield as they climbed to safety on the roof. It might have been a good plan, but they would never know, because the pig had stepped on the main door-locking button and locked itself in.

And the key was still in the ignition.

Franck Mingeaut calmly pulled a mobile phone from the inside pocket of his jacket, then feverishly dialed 18, the emergency number.

When the firemen arrived, the pig had settled down. Well, somewhat. Fact is, there wasn't anything left for it to smash.

The fire chief walked around the car, visibly impressed. He couldn't help saying, "Such a beautiful car. Breaks your heart, eh?"

What happened next is unbearable for people who love beautiful things.

One of the men fetched an enormous rifle, like a bazooka. He waved everybody aside and took aim. The pig and the window exploded at the same time.

The inside of the car got a new paint job: red.

There was blood everywhere, deep in the glove compartment and between the keys on the car phone.

Alexandre Devermont was stunned. You might have thought he'd stopped thinking. Completely. About anything. Or only about burying himself alive, or turning the fireman's bazooka on himself.

You'd be wrong. Actually, he was thinking about gossip in the area and the godsend this would be for the conservationists.

It should be said that his father had not only a magnificent Jaguar but also tenacious political designs aimed at thwarting the Greens.

Because the Greens want to outlaw hunting and create a nature reserve and whatever else they can, so long as it pisses off the big landowners.

It's a battle papa is deeply committed to and one that until now he'd almost won. Just last night, as he was carving a duck at the dinner table, he'd said, "Hey! Here's one that Grolet and his gang of tight-asses won't be watching in their binoculars anymore! Ha, ha, ha!"

But now . . . a wild pig blown to bits inside the future regional counselor's Jaguar Sovereign, that was sure to make things a bit awkward, wasn't it?

There were even hairs plastered against the windows.

The firemen left, the cops left. Tomorrow a tow truck would come to load up the . . . the . . . well, the hunk of gray metal cluttering the roadway.

Our two pals are walking down the road, tuxedo jackets slung over their shoulders. There's nothing to say. In any case, the way things stand, it isn't even worth thinking anymore, either.

"Want a cigarette?" says Franck.

"Sure," Alexandre answers.

They walk along like that for a long time. The sun rises over the fields, the sky is pink, a few stars linger a while longer. There isn't a sound to be heard, just a rustling in the grass from the rabbits running in the ditches.

Then Alexandre Devermont turns to his friend and says, "So what about that blonde you were telling me about? The one with the big tits. Who is she?"

And his friend smiles at him.

Translated by William Rodarmor

Clochemerle

Gabriel Chevallier

TO THE WEST of the Route Nationale No. 6, which goes from Lyon to Paris, there lies, between Arise and the outskirts of Macon over a distance of about forty-five kilometers, a region which shares with Burgundy, Anjou, Bordelais, and the Côtes du Rhone, the honor of producing the most celebrated wines in France. The names of Brouilly, Morgon, Julienas, and Moulin-à-Vent have made Beaujolais famous. But side by side with these names there are others, with less splendor attaching to them, which are yet indicative of substantial merits. In the forefront of those names from which an unjust fate has withheld a widespread renown comes that of Clochemerle-en-Beaujolais.

GABRIEL CHEVALLIER (1895–1969) will forever be associated with his 1934 comic masterpiece, *Clochemerle*. A tale of high and low jinks in a French village, the book has sold millions of copies and been translated into more than twenty languages. Though Chevallier's classic holds his invented village up to ridicule, several French towns have claimed to be its model. (For the record, it was inspired by Vaux-en-Beaujolais, which is fifty kilometers northeast of Lyon.) Jocelyn Godefroi's translation was published in England in 1952.

Let us explain this name of Clochemerle. In the twelfth century, before the vine was in cultivation there, this district, which was under the sway of the lords of Beaujeu, was a thickly wooded region. The site of the present town was occupied by an abbey—which, by the way, is in itself an assurance that it was well chosen. The abbey church— of which there still remain, blended with the structures of later periods, a doorway, a charming bell turret, some Romanesque arches and solid walls—was surrounded by very large trees, and in these trees blackbirds built their nests. When the bell was rung the blackbirds would fly away. The peasants of that period spoke of "the blackbirds' bell," *la cloche à merles*. The name has remained.

One thing is certain, that Beaujolais is insufficiently known by epicures for the quality of its wine and by tourists as a district. As a vintage, it is sometimes regarded as a mere appendage to Burgundy, like the tail of a comet, so to speak. There is a tendency among all those who live far from the Department of the Rhône to believe that Morgon is but a pale imitation of Gorton. This is a gross and unpardonable error, committed by people who drink with no power of discrimination, trusting to a mere label or to some headwaiter's questionable assertions. Few drinkers of wine are qualified, with the filched trademarks on the bottle caps, to distinguish between what is genuine and what is not. In reality, the Beaujolais wine has its own peculiar merits and a flavor which cannot be confused with that of any other wine.

The great tourist crowd does not visit this wine-growing country. This is due to its situation. While Burgundy, between Beaune and Dijon, displays its hills on either

side of the same Route Nationale No. 6 which extends
along the edge of the Beaujolais country, this latter region
comprises a series of hills situated at a distance from the
main roads, completely covered with vineyards to a height
varying from seven hundred to sixteen hundred feet, their
highest summits, which shelter the district from the west
winds, attaining a height of over three thousand feet. Set
apart in these hills, which act as a succession of screens,
the towns and villages of Beaujolais, with their healthy,
bracing air, enjoy an isolated position and retain a flavor
of feudal times.

But the tourist blindly follows the Saône valley—and
a pleasant one it is—ignorant of the fact that he is leaving
behind him, only a few kilometers away, one of the sun-
niest and most picturesque corners of France. Thus it is
that Beaujolais is still a district reserved for a tiny number
of enthusiasts who come there for the sake of its restful
peace and its far-flung, distant views, while the Sunday
drivers rev their engines so they may race ahead to the
most popular, overcrowded spots.

It was the month of October 1922, at about five o'clock
in the afternoon. The principal square of Clochemerle-
en-Beaujolais was shady with its great chestnuts, in the
center of which stood a magnificent lime tree said to have
been planted in 1518 to celebrate the arrival of Anne de
Beaujeu in those parts. Two men were strolling up and
down together with the unhurried gait of country people
who seem to have unlimited time to give to everything.
There was such emphatic precision in all that they were
saying to each other that they spoke only after long intervals of preparation—barely one sentence for every twenty

steps. Frequently a single word, or an exclamation, served for a whole sentence; but these exclamations conveyed shades of meaning that were full of significance for two speakers who were very old acquaintances united in the pursuit of common aims and in laying the foundations of a cherished scheme. At that moment they were exercised in mind over worries of municipal origin, in which they were having to contend with opposition. And this it was that made them so solemn and so discreet.

One of these men, past fifty years of age, tall, fair-haired, of sanguine complexion, could have been taken for a typical descendant of the Burgundians who formerly inhabited the department of the Rhône. His face, the skin of which was indented by exposure to sun and wind, owed its expression almost entirely to his small, light grey eyes, which were surrounded by tiny wrinkles, and which he was perpetually blinking; this gave him an air of roguishness, harsh at times and at others friendly. His mouth, which might have given indications of character that could not be read in his eyes, was entirely hidden by his drooping mustache, beneath which was thrust the stem of a short black pipe, smelling of a mixture of tobacco and of dried grape skins, which he chewed at rather than smoked. Thin and gaunt, with long, straight legs, and a slight paunch which was more the outcome of lack of exercise than a genuine stoutness, the man gave an impression of a powerful physique. Although carelessly dressed, from his comfortable, well-polished shoes, the good quality of the cloth of his coat, and the collar which he wore with natural ease on a weekday, you guessed that he was respected and well-to-do. His

voice and his sparing use of gesture were those of a man
accustomed to rule.

His name was Barthélemy Piéchut. He was mayor
of the town of Clochemerle, where he was the principal
vine-grower, owning the best slopes with southwesterly
aspect, those which produce the richest wines. In addition
to this, he was president of the agricultural syndicate and
a departmental councillor, which made him an important personage over a district of several square miles at
Salles, Odenas, Arbuissons, Vaux, and Perreon. He was
commonly supposed to have other political aims not yet
revealed. People envied him, but his influential position
was gratifying to the countryside. On his head he wore
only the peasant's black felt hat, tilted back, with the
crown dented inwards and the wide brim trimmed with
braid. His hands clutched the inside of his waistcoat and
his head was bent forward. This was his customary attitude
when deciding difficult questions, and much impressed
the inhabitants. "He's thinking hard, old Piéchut!" they
would say.

His interlocutor, on the other hand, was a puny indi-
vidual, whose age it would have been impossible to guess.
His goatee beard concealed a notably receding chin,
while over an imposing cartilage serving as an armored
protection for a pair of resonant tubes which imparted a
nasal intonation to all his remarks, he wore old-fashioned
spectacles with unplated frames, kept in place by a small
chain attached to his ear. Behind these glasses, which his
short sight demanded, the glint of his sea-green eyes was
of the kind that denotes a mind given over to wild fancies and occupied in dreaming of the ways and means to

an unattainable ideal. His bony head was adorned with a Panama hat, which, as the result of exposure to the sun for several summers and storage in a cupboard in winter, had acquired the tint and the crackly nature of those sheaves of Indian corn which, hanging to dry, are a common sight in the Bresse country under the projecting roofs of the farms. His shoes, on which the exercise of the shoe-maker's skill was only too conspicuous, were reaching the period of their final resoling, for it was becoming unlikely that a new piece would rescue the uppers, now definitely breathing their last. The man was sucking at a very mea-ger cigarette, richer in paper than tobacco, and clumsily rolled. This other personage was Ernest Tafardel, school-master, town clerk, and consequently right-hand man to Barthélemy Piéchut, his confidant at certain seasons, but to a limited extent only (for the mayor never went far in his confidences, and never farther than he had decided to go); and lastly, his adviser in the case of administrative correspondence of a complicated nature.

For the smaller details of material existence, the school-master displayed the lofty detachment of the true intel-lectual. "A fine intelligence," he would say, "can dispense with polished shoes." By this metaphor he intended to convey that splendor in dress, or mediocrity, can neither add to nor detract from a man's intelligence. This bore the further implication that at Clochemerle there was to be found at least one fine intelligence—unhappily con-fined to a subordinate role—the possessor of which could be recognized by the poverty-stricken appearance of his shoes. For Ernest Tafardel was vain enough to regard himself as a profound thinker, a sort of rustic philosopher, ascetic and misunderstood. Every utterance of his had a pedagogic, sententious twist, and was punctuated at frequent intervals by the gesture which, in pictures that used to be sold to the populace, was assigned to members of the teaching body—a forefinger held vertically above the closed fist raised to the level of the face. Whenever he made a statement, Ernest Tafardel would press his forefinger to his nose with such force as to displace the point of it. It was, therefore, hardly surprising that after twenty years of a profession in which affirmative statements are constantly required, his nose had become slightly deflected to the left. To complete this portrait, it must be added that the schoolmaster's fine maxims were spoiled by the quality of his breath, with the result that the people of Clochemerle fought shy of his wise utterances, which were wafted toward his hearers at too close quarters. As he was the only person throughout the countryside to be unconscious of this unpleasant defect, the haste with which the inhabitants of Clochemerle would flee from him, and above all their eagerness to cut short every confidential conversation or impassioned dispute, was attributed by him to ignorance and base materialism on their part. When people simply gave way to him and fled without further argument, Tafardel suspected them of despising him. Thus his feeling of persecution rested upon a misunderstanding. Nevertheless, it caused him real suffering, for, being naturally prolix, as a well-informed man he would have liked to make a display of his learning. He concluded from this isolation of his that the race of mountain wine growers had, as the result of fifteen centuries of religious and feudal oppression, grown addlepated.

He revenged himself by the keen hatred he bore toward Ponosse, the parish priest—a hatred which, however, was platonic and based on purely doctrinal grounds.

A follower of Epictetus and Jean-Jacques Rousseau, the schoolmaster led a blameless life, devoting his whole leisure to municipal correspondence and to drawing up statements which he sent to the *Vintners' Gazette* of Belleville-sur-Saône. Though he had lost his wife many years previously, his morals remained above suspicion. A native of the Lozère, a district noted for its austerity, Tafardel had been unable to accustom himself to the coarse jesting of wine bibbers. These barbarians, he thought, were flouting science and progress in his own person. For these reasons he felt the more gratitude and devotion to Barthélemy Piéchut, whose attitude toward him was one of sympathy and trust. But the mayor was a clever fellow, who knew how to turn everything and everybody to good account. Whenever he was to have a serious conversation with the schoolmaster, he would take him out for a walk; by this means, he always got him in profile. It must also be remembered that the distance which separates a schoolmaster from a large landed proprietor placed between them a trench, dug by deference, which put the mayor beyond reach of those emanations which Tafardel bestowed so freely when directly facing people of lesser importance. Lastly, like the good politician that he was, Piéchut turned to his own advantage his secretary's pestiferous exhalations. If, in some troublesome matter, he wished to obtain the approval of certain municipal councilors of the opposition, the notary Girodot, or the wine growers Lamolire and Maniguant, he pretended to be indisposed and sent Tafardel, with his papers and his odorous eloquence, to their respective houses. To close the schoolmaster's mouth, they gave their consent. The unfortunate Tafardel imagined himself endowed with quite exceptional powers of argument—a conviction which consoled him for his social setbacks, which he attributed to the envy aroused in the hearts of mediocre persons by contact with superior ability. It was a very proud man that returned from these missions. Barthélemy Piéchut smiled unobtrusively and, rubbing the red nape of his neck, a sign with him either of deep reflection or of great joy, he would say to the schoolmaster:

"You would have made a fine diplomat, Tafardel. You've only to open your mouth and everyone agrees with you."

"Monsieur le Maire," Tafardel would reply, "that is the advantage of learning. There is a way of putting a case which is beyond the capacity of the ignorant, but which always succeeds in winning them over."

At the moment when this story begins, Barthélemy Piéchut was making this pronouncement:

"We must think of something, Tafardel, which will be a shining example of the superiority of a progressive town council."

"I entirely agree with you, Monsieur Piéchut. But I must point out that there is already the war memorial."

"There will soon be one in every town, whatever sort of council it may have. We must find something more original, more in keeping with the party program. Don't you agree?"

"Of course, of course, Monsieur Piéchut. We have got to bring progress into the country districts and wage war unceasingly on obscurantism. That is the great task for all us men of the Left."

They ceased speaking and made their way across the square, a distance of about eighty yards, halting where it ended in a terrace and commanded a view over the first valley. Behind lay a confused mass of other valleys formed by the slopes of rounded hills that fell away to the level of the plain of the Saône, which could be seen in a blue haze in the far distance. The heat of that month of October gave more body to the odor of new wine that floated over the whole countryside. The mayor asked:

"Have you an idea, Tafardel?"

"An idea, Monsieur Piéchut, an idea?"

They resumed their walk. The schoolmaster was nodding his head in contemplative fashion. He raised his hat, which had shrunk through old age and was pressing on his temples. Then he replaced it carefully. When they had covered the whole distance, the mayor began again: "Yes, an idea. Have you one, Tafardel?"

"Well, Monsieur Piéchut . . . there is a matter that occurred to me the other day. I was intending to speak to you about it. The cemetery belongs, I take it, to the town? It is, in fact, a public monument?"

"Certainly, Tafardel."

"In that case, why is it the only public monument in Clochemerle which does not bear the Republican motto —'Liberty, Equality, and Fraternity'? Is that not an oversight which plays into the hands of the reactionaries and the curé? Does it not look like an admission on the part of the Republic that its supervision comes to an end at the threshold of eternity? Does it not amount to a confession that the dead escape from the jurisdiction of the parties of the Left? The strength of priests, Monsieur Piéchut, lies in their monopoly of the dead. It is of the greatest importance to show that we, too, hold rights over them."

These words were followed by a momentous silence, devoted to an examination of this suggestion. Then the mayor replied, in a brisk, friendly tone:

"Do you want to know what I think, Tafardel? The dead are the dead. Let us leave them in peace."

"There is no question of disturbing them, but only of protecting them against the abuses of reaction. For after all, the separation of Church and State . . ."

"It's no use, Tafardel! No. We should only be saddling ourselves with a troublesome business that interests nobody and would have a bad effect. You can't stop the curé from going into the cemetery, can you? Or from doing it more often than other people? Well . . . any inscription we might put up on the walls . . . And then the dead, Tafardel—they belong to the past. It is the future that we have to think of. It's some plan for the future that I am asking you for."

"In that case, Monsieur Piéchut, I return to my proposal for a municipal library, where we should have a choice of books capable of enlarging the people's minds and of dealing a final blow at past fanaticisms."

"Don't let us waste our time over this library business. I have already told you—the people of Clochemerle won't read those books of yours. The newspaper is ample for their needs. Do you suppose that they read much? Your scheme would give us a great deal of trouble without doing us much good. What we need is something that will make a greater effect, and be in keeping with a time of progress like the present. Then you can think of absolutely nothing?"

"I shall give my mind to it, Monsieur le Maire. Should I be indiscreet in asking whether you yourself—"

"Yes, Tafardel, I have an idea. I've been thinking it over for a long time."

"Ah, good, good!" the schoolmaster replied.

But he asked no question. For there is nothing else which destroys so effectively, in a native of Clochemerle, all inclination to speak. Tafardel did not even betray any curiosity. He contented himself with merely showing confident approval:

"If you have an idea, there is no need to inquire any further!"

Thereupon Barthélemy Piéchut halted in the middle of the square, near the lime tree, while he glanced toward the main street in order to make sure that no one was coming in their direction. Then he placed his hand on the nape of his neck and moved it upward until his hat became tilted forward over his eyes. There he remained, staring at the ground, and gently rubbing the back of his head. Finally, he made up his mind:

"I am going to tell you what my idea is, Tafardel. I want to put up a building at the town's expense."

"At the town's expense?" the schoolmaster repeated in astonishment, knowing what a source of unpopularity a raid on the common fund derived from taxes can be.

But he made no inquiry as to the kind of building, nor what sum would have to be spent. He knew the mayor for a man of great common sense, cautious and very shrewd.

And it was the mayor himself who, of his own accord, proceeded to clear the matter up:

"Yes, a building—and a useful one, too, from the point of view of the public health as well as public morals. Now let us see if you are clever, Tafardel. Have a guess."

Ernest Tafardel moved his arms in a gesture indicating how vast was the sphere of conjecture, and that it would be folly to embark on it. Piéchut gave a final tilt to his hat, which threw his face completely into shadow, blinked his eyes—the right one a little more than the left—to get a clear conception of the impression that his idea would make on his hearer, and then laid the whole matter bare:

"I want to build a urinal, Tafardel."

"A urinal?" the schoolmaster cried out, startled and impressed. The matter, he saw at once, was obviously of extreme importance.

The mayor had a wrong impression of what this exclamation conveyed.

"Yes, a public convenience," he said.

"Oh, I quite understood, Monsieur Piéchut."

"Well, what about it?"

Now, when a matter of such consequence is revealed to you suddenly and without warning, you cannot produce a readymade opinion regarding it. And at Clochemerle, precipitancy detracts from the value of a judgment. As though for the purpose of seeing clearly into his own mind, with a lively jerk Tafardel unsaddled his large, equine nose and held his spectacles to his mouth, where he imbued them with fetid moisture, and then, rubbing them with his handkerchief, gave them a new transparence. Having assured himself that no further specks of dust remained on the glasses, he replaced them with a solemnity that denoted the exceptional importance of the interview. These precautions delighted Piéchut; they showed him that his confidences were producing an effect on his hearer. Twice or thrice more there came a *Hum!* from Tafardel from behind his thin, ink-stained hand, whilst he stroked his old nanny-goat beard. Then he said:

"A really fine idea, Monsieur le Maire! An idea worthy of a good republican, and altogether in keeping with the spirit of the party. Egalitarian in every sense, and hygienic, too, as you so justly pointed out. And when one thinks that the great nobles under Louis the XIV used to relieve themselves on the palace staircases! A fine thing to happen in the times of the monarchy, you may well say! A urinal, and one of Ponosse's processions—from the point of view of public welfare you simply could not compare them."

"And how about Girodot," the mayor asked, "and Lamolire, and Maniguant, the whole gang in fact—do you think they will be knocked flat?"

Thereupon was heard the little grating noise that was the schoolmaster's substitute for laughter; it was a rare manifestation with this sad, misunderstood personage whose joy in life was so tainted, and was reserved exclusively for good objects and great occasions, the winning of victories over the distressing obscurantism with which the French countryside is even now infected. And such victories are rare.

"No doubt of it, no doubt of it, Monsieur Piéchut. Your plan will do them an immense amount of damage in the eyes of the public."

"And what of Saint-Ghoul? And Baroness Courtebiche?"

"It may well be the deathblow to what little remains of the prestige of the nobility! It will be a splendid democratic victory, a fresh affirmation of immortal principles. Have you spoken of it to the Committee?"

"Not yet . . . there are jealousies there. . . . I am rather counting on your eloquence, Tafardel, to explain the matter and carry it through. You're such an expert at shutting up grousers!"

"You may rely on me, Monsieur le Maire."

"Well, then, that's settled. We will choose a day. For the moment, not a word! I rather think that, for once in a way, we are going to have an amusing time!"

"I think so, too, Monsieur Piéchut!"

In his contentment, the mayor kept turning his hat round on his head in every direction. Still greedy for compliments, to extract fresh ones he made little exclamations to the schoolmaster, such as "Well?" "Now just tell me!" in the sly, cunning manner of the peasant, whilst he continually rubbed the nape of his neck, which appeared to be the seat of his mental activity. Each exclamation was answered by Tafardel with some fresh eulogy.

It was the loveliest moment of the day, an autumn evening of rare beauty. The air was filled with the shrill cries of birds returning to roost, while an all-pervading calm was shed upon the earth from the heavens above, where a tender blue was gently turning to the rose-pink which heralds a splendid twilight. The sun was disappearing behind the mountains of Azergues, and its light now fell only upon a few peaks which still emerged from the surrounding ocean of gentle calm and rural peace, and upon scattered points in the crowded plain of the Saône, where its last rays formed pools of light. The harvest had been a good one, the wine promised to be of excellent quality. There was cause for rejoicing in that corner of Beaujolais. Clochemerle re-echoed with the noise of the shifting of casks. Puffs of cool air from the stillrooms, bearing a slightly acid smell, cut across the warm atmosphere of the square when the chestnuts were rustling in the northeasterly breeze. Everywhere stains from the winepress were to be seen and already the brandy was in the process of being distilled.

Standing at the edge of the terrace, the two men were gazing at the peaceful decline of day. This apotheosis of the dying summer season appeared to them in the light of a happy omen. Suddenly, with a touch of pomposity, Tafardel asked:

"By the way, Monsieur le Maire, where are we going to place our little edifice? Have you thought of that?"

A rich smile, in which every wrinkle on his face was involved, overspread the mayor's countenance. All the same his jovial expression was somehow menacing. It was a smile that afforded an admirable illustration of the famous political maxim—"To govern is to foresee." In that smile of Barthélemy Piéchut's could be read the satisfaction he felt in his consciousness of power, in the fear he inspired, and in his ownership of lovely sun-warmed vineyards and of cellars which housed the best of the wines grown on the slopes that lay between the mountain passes of the West and the low ground of Brouilly. With this smile, the natural accompaniment of a successful life, he enveloped the excitable, highly-strung Tafardel—a poor devil who had not a patch of ground nor a strip of vineyard to his name—with the pity felt by men of action for poor feeble scribblers who waste their time over vaporous nonsense. Happily for himself, the schoolmaster was protected from the shafts of irony by his fervor in a good cause and his belief in missions undertaken in the name of freedom. Nothing could wound his pride except the inexplicable recoil of his interlocutors when face-to-face with his corrosive aphorisms. The mayor's presence filled his whole being with the warmth of human kindliness, and kept alight within his heart the sacred fire of his self-esteem. At that moment he was awaiting a reply from the man of whom the people of Clochemerle were wont to say: "Piéchut doesn't wear out his tongue for nothing!" He did not do so now.

"Come and let us see the place, Tafardel!" he said simply, making his way toward the main street.

A great utterance. The utterance of a man who has made every decision in advance. An utterance comparable with Napoleon's when crossing the fields of Austerlitz: "Here, I shall give battle."

To make the urinal of general utility, it had to be situated in an easily accessible spot which would not be more advantageous to one portion of the town than the other. The best solution would undoubtedly have been to provide three equidistant urinals, allotted respectively to the upper, lower, and center parts of the town. The mayor had not lost sight of this possibility. But, for a newly conceived plan, this would have meant playing for stakes altogether too high. By exercising prudence he might well make a success; but if his ideas were on too ambitious a scale, he would only be inviting his enemies to charge him with extravagance, and exposing himself to great unpopularity. A place like Clochemerle, which had done without a urinal for a thousand years and more, hardly felt a need suddenly to possess three, particularly if it had to pay for them. And still less so, if it be remembered that the use of the urinal would involve some preliminary education for the inhabitants, possibly even a municipal decree. Men who from generation to generation had relieved themselves against the foot of a wall or in hollows in the ground, with that fine freedom of action which the Clochemerle wine confers (it is reputed to be good for the kidneys), would be but little inclined to overflow at a spot predetermined and lacking in all those small pleasures that are to be found in the indulgence of such little whims and fancies, as that of a jet well aimed that drives away a greenfly, bends a blade of grass, drowns an ant, or tracks down a spider in his web. In the country, where diversions are few and far between, even the most trivial pleasures must be taken into account. And taken into account, also, must be the male privilege of doing this in an upright position, openly and merrily; which gives the men some prestige in the eyes of the women.

Translated by Jocelyn Godefroi

It Was Yesterday

Annie Saumont

SCORCHED EARTH. The grass grew back afterward.
She says, Marc don't go into the blackberries. An isolated
oppidum dominating the valleys. Only one way in, from
the East. For defense, it's better than Gergovia, better
than Avaricum. She says, Marc, stop teasing your brother.
I didn't do anything. To Victor. He's such a crybaby.

Caesar began the siege of Alesia in 52 BC. Where were
you during the war? Red hair blazing in the sunlight, he
doesn't even turn his head. Come on, move, we're in a
hurry. You promised you would show me the place. The

ANNIE SAUMONT (1927–) is France's best-known writer
of short stories. She is also the translator of many books from
English, including *The Catcher in the Rye*. In addition to J. D.
Salinger, she has translated V. S. Naipaul, Nadine Gordimer,
John Fowles, Michael Dorris, and Sandra Cisneros. Saumont
won the short-story Prix Goncourt for *Quelquefois dans les céré-
monies* (1981) and the Prix de l'Académie Française in 2003 for
the whole of her work. Her many books include *Je suis pas un
camion* (1989, tr. *I'm No Truck*), *Noir, comme d'habitude* (2000),
Koman sa sécri émé? (2005), and *Les croissants du dimanche* (2008).
This story is from *Moi les enfants j'aime pas tellement* (2001).

real one. Because that stuff back there on the TV, that was a joke. She reassures him, it's higher up, we'll cut across the meadow.

But you've got to say, too, grandma, tell us. Can you explain it to me, grandma? Now that I'm seven. Did the Romans drive their tanks to the parking lot where you left your car? There weren't any tanks in that war, little guy.

Tanks, that was the last time. Only about forty years ago. Yesterday. The tanks rolled through the valley, friends or enemies, we didn't know. And the redheaded boy on the sidewalk against the wall and the poster NOTICE TO THE POPULATION, BY ORDER OF — watching as the man in the black uniform toppled onto the wet flagstones, then watching the thin trickle of blood run into the gutter. On the other side of the street the girl still out of breath, wearing her dirty wrinkled blue dress, frozen as if forever. But the scene is already coming to life, the girl opens her mouth but only a strangled hiccup comes out. The man holding the rifle calmly says, Go home, kids.

Proconsul Julius Caesar arranged his troops with the care of a great strategist. Four cohorts of legionnaires in each of the twenty-three forts. Seventy thousand soldiers. Caesar planned to starve the town out. Though unruly by nature, the Gauls accept the ferocious discipline their leader imposes. Where were you during the war? What war? The war when our country was called Gaul and the people were the Gauls. Oh, that was so long ago. Twenty centuries. When Vercingetorix—his name means king of warriors—assembled the Celtic army. Afterward there were other wars.

The child looked up, then nodded, shaking his red

locks, there was the Jerusalem artichoke and the rutabaga war, when boys his age were only too happy to eat them —isn't that so, grandma, you said so. And that's why you scold me when I leave stuff on my plate. Yes, grandma, you already told us about the time when children had never seen an orange. She won't add—as she drives her two little grandsons comfortably settled in the back seat of the white Austin home from a vacation in the sun—she won't add that in those days fifteen-year-old boys carried scraps of rolled-up paper in their bicycle handlebars, tracts and messages for the mimeo machine. It was yesterday. The time of dangerous games, of risky meetings. She was shivering in her light blue dress, but he'd said that she looked good in blue. He said, Tomorrow at five, and it must be about six now, she guessed, she doesn't have a watch, the church clock always read twelve, ever since the clockmaker was executed in front of the portal. A terrorist, they'd called him. The redheaded boy's mother had cried that day, she told him, Don't ever get mixed up in that stuff or I'll lock you in the shed. Six thirty. Maybe seven. My God they've arrested him, or else his mother locked him up. And suddenly there he is, pushing his bike, blazing red hair narrow shoulders arms and legs that go on forever. Freckles on his nose. She loves him. Hey, grandma, tell us. Why did Caesar come to Gaul, since he was the chief back home in a nice sunny country? Because people always want things they don't have. Victor—who's three—trips on the roots, she picks him up, helps him over the obstacle. Me, says Marc, I just want a gas station, a pinball machine, and a box of Legos and an Indian tepee, and roller skates and a record player, and— Oh stop. Yeah, well that's all.

This year the raspberry bushes have grown over the path that Marc is setting out on. Raspberries and blackberries. The vegetable turbulence escapes the control of the ministry of historic sites and will stealthily continue to blot out landmarks, restoring some wildness to the world. One spring day when he turns fifteen, this redheaded boy will think he's alone on earth, alone with a girl his age he will have begged or cajoled into coming into the woods with him. You and I, it was yesterday. The time was past for modesty, for whispered words and innocent caresses, we were about undressing, talking with our soft, feverish, awkward bodies. That was the moment you tore me, for days and weeks until the blood flowed again I was so afraid I was pregnant with a valiant little warrior fathered at Alesia.

ALESIA HISTORIC SITE. Now, there was a clearly visible sign by the highway that you had to exit farther on, at the Semur-en-Auxois junction. After eight kilometers on the departmental road you crossed the city with its towers and ramparts. Then another fifteen kilometers up the valley and you could see the roofs of Alise-Sainte-Reine. Victor had waited too long before asking for a pee stop, it never failed. We stopped at the parking lot. Vic writhing in the back seat, his hand between his thighs. Marc said, You know, grandma, this little pig got the rug all wet. And then asking for the first time, feverishly, Is it here that Julius Caesar's soldiers parked their tanks?

There weren't any tanks in those days, darling, the weapons were bows and arrows, and also catapults javelins lances. Get out, you two. Wait, Victor. Go ahead.

Hurry up. Then Victor put dirt in his mouth. He stood there, cheeks swollen, tears in his eyes, Spit it out said Marc, spit it out, Victor, or else you'll be poisoned and die. And dying hurts. It hurts so much that often you can't move at all anymore.

You so tall at fifteen so thin and as if petrified, you against the wall near the plaque with the writing—it must have been the name of the street. Yellow stucco. A streak of rust running down from the edge of the plaque. Below, the rust of your hair. With a head of hair like that, you could hardly pass unnoticed. And the man, hidden in the corner of a porch—a bald guy with very pale eyes—later said he wasn't about to let them kill the reddest redhead anyone had ever seen. A direct descendant of Vercingetorix, she'd once claimed. Everyone knows that Vercingetorix had a reddish mustache and surely the same color hair, but you never saw it under his helmet. Yes, Marc, that's who you get your copper-colored hair from. And why isn't Vic a redhead? Vic took after the Roman side. Because afterward, there were marriages.

You idiot. You're saying anything at all. Damned kids, they always have to be talking and asking questions. Like earlier at the Beaune turnoff, where they'd opened a museum. With the beating of drums on the soundtrack, a video showed the series of battles during the siege of Alesia. Grandma, so the yellow squares, those are the Romans? Yes, and the blue circles are the Gauls. Look, grandma, the yellow circles are advancing, no, I don't wanna, shouted Marc. Through the panoramic window you could see the wooden fortifications, the earthen berms, the double trench, and the slope with its mantraps.

Turris pinna vallum, faithful reconstitution according to Caesar's writings. Oh, the poor Gauls, whimpered Marc as the blue marbles rushed together chaotically for the final battle. Grandma, you would've wanted the Gauls to win, too. Wouldn't you? Tell me. You have to answer children's questions even when you're thinking of something else. Even amid this rush of memories when it's fall and you can again wander through the woods with no risk of running into militia patrols. It was yesterday. Reddish curls, burnished gold of the oaks. Take your little brother by the hand, we'll climb the embankment, upsy-daisy. But if we go too far, grandma—then we'll be lost in the forest of the storybooks we'll eat wild fruits and roots. We'll make a fire, the boy said, to keep wild animals away. No sooner said than done. The teenager with the red hair puts his words into action, bluish-gray smoke rises straight up toward the dark blue sky, his trembling hand stroking the blouse she will soon dare to remove. And the little boy—seven, already—if grandpa were here we wouldn't be so afraid. And again, for the hundredth time, why did he go away?

You can't explain that grandpa also wanted to return to his youth (it was yesterday). That's why he chose to go live with Florence who isn't even as old as your mother, little guy. And grandpa rides a bicycle. That's what he likes to remember. You can't make a seven-year-old child understand that. Listen, Marc, grandpa hasn't really gone away, since you see him every month. But gone away from your house, said Marc, And you don't see him anymore, grandma.

No. But she meets him here. The teenager roaming the

woods in the Alise-Sainte-Reine hills. The boy who was a refugee from the Ardennes, like her. At first people in Burgundy said that they came from somewhere else, that they were strangers. Then people forgot. She was the well-behaved girl who lodged at the baker's and was studying for her diploma. He was the young boy who rode his poor squeaky bike to the lycée every day and never refused a mission, who knew how to keep quiet, the one the SS man's rifle was aimed at and then another rifle shot the SS man in black just as he was about to fire. The following month the war was over. Two thousand years earlier, criers stationed along the roads would have used their lungs to spread the news. Where were you during the war. Which war. You know, that one.

I was— but she didn't say anything. I was standing on the sidewalk. I was the girl in the blue dress—motionless—barely fifteen, eyes bulging, a hand over my mouth to stifle a scream. Then the other man said, Go home, kids. As if nothing had happened.

ALESIA HISTORIC SITE. Well, look, here we are. No don't climb on the bench, come with me to the hilltop, you'll see the statue of the great warrior much better from there. He was a giant, don't cry Vic, he isn't mean, said Marc, I even think he's handsome. Vic, are you glad we came? Vic thought we would also see the big horse and that we'd ride horsy, you're crazy it would be too high you'd fall, so now you're crying again, say Vic, why do you always— Leave him alone, poor kid, I'll carry him, let's go down the wooden stairway, we'll get the car and we'll be home in a jiffy. We'll give this baby some soup and put him to bed. Then you and I will have a quiet dinner. Me and you, said the boy, we won't go to bed early, we'll talk, we'll talk about the war. Which war? The war between the Gauls and the Romans. Because your war, grandma, he sighs, shakes his red curls, because your war is no fun. He hesitates. Tries to think for a moment. He gets angry, makes up his mind, When you tell it, your war, it's like it was very far away, see.

Translated by William Rodarmor

The Dogs in Our Life

Marcel Aymé

YES, I'LL TELL YOU the story of the dogs, but first, take off your clogs. Just as I thought—they're full of snow! And your socks, look what a state they're in! If you hadn't dawdled along the way, you'd have come home with dry feet; but no, you'd rather go stomping about with those other little rascals. People told me they saw all of you sliding in the hollow one day, and right in the steepest part. Oh, if I'd known! When I think of your mother, poor little lamb, I can see her in my mind's eye, so sweet and dependable! She was never one to slide in the hollow! Winter or summer, she'd make it home from school in barely a quarter of an hour. And it takes you forty-five minutes, sometimes

---

MARCEL AYMÉ (1902–1967) was a popular author of novels, plays, and short stories whose politics—or lack of them—managed to irritate friend and foe alike. During the Occupation, for example, he made movies with a Marxist director while writing stories for collaborationist publications. Aymé wrote in the realistic vein of a Balzac or a Zola while leaving room for playful, ironic fantasy, as in his most famous work, *Le passe-muraille* (1943, tr. *The Walker-Through-Walls*). This story is from his 1950 collection, *En arrière*.

more—and with your feet wet, or even your clothes all torn, like the day before yesterday. It's enough to make me not want to tell you about the dogs. Go set your clogs on the oven, and then come sit here in front of the stove, and put your feet up on the hob.

Now, the first dog we had here was one I brought with me in 1909, when I came to my new home. My father had set him aside for me when his Musette had puppies at the end of autumn, seven or eight months before my wedding. The dog's name was Pyramus. He was iron gray, with short hair and upright ears, not too big, and not too nice-looking, either. He was a good herding dog, and a good watchdog, too, affectionate at heart. When he was young he loved to play, and the two of us—I was twenty—we'd have a grand old time. But for all that, he favored your grandfather, who wasn't even nice to him. You'd find no better man in the whole town than my poor Hector, but he had no qualms about kicking a dog. He beat Pyramus more than once. Of course, Pyramus really deserved it, being a bit of a thief, and always getting in the way of our work—standing right at our legs and putting on important airs, as if all our chores had to go through him first. He was always there when we least needed him. Once when I was carrying some *cabuchon* dough out to the oven, that dog tripped me in the middle of the courtyard and I fell face first into the dough! Oh, was I ever mad!

Another thing about Pyramus: he was vicious to everyone but us. He couldn't stand it when people came over; he would bark at them endlessly, teeth bared, with a mean look in his eyes. I was always afraid he'd bite someone, as happened so many times, not people but other dogs, which he also couldn't stand. In the pasture, too, when he was watching over the cows, he was fierce and furious; he always had to have the last word. There was one testy cow, called Brunette, I think, who would charge him, horns lowered. Many dogs, if a cow confronts them, they run off; you'll see them cowering, their tails between their legs and their backs rounded. But Pyramus, he'd stand his ground, and it was always the cow that backed down.

That's how he was, and at the mere sound of his gruff and menacing bark, people coming down the road would veer away. For him what mattered was the family—his master, me, and the two children we'd had by then: your uncle Francis, who was born in April 1911, and your mother, poor lamb, born in November of the following year. No dog was sweeter or more patient with the two little ones than he. They could pull his hair, his tail, his ears all they wanted and he wouldn't flinch; but if anyone so much as came near them, he'd growl and look mean. He loved his house and his family so much that you'd never see him roaming around like the other dogs. He always had to be right there, in the courtyard or out with the cows in the pasture or in the kitchen, as if we wouldn't have been able to do without him. But anytime your grandfather went out, whether to get a pack of tobacco at La Frisée's or, on Sundays, to play *quilles*, Pyramus would follow right at his heels, proud and happy as could be.

And then, in 1914, it was an August day, I remember— the fields across the road were ready for harvesting— Hector went off to the war. He didn't want me to go with him to the train at Mont-sous-Vaudrey. He kissed the children good-bye, and to console me, he said he'd be back in three weeks. He headed down the road, and when he got to the big beech tree, he sent Pyramus home; the dog had followed him. Pyramus returned contritely. He didn't yet realize that his master would be gone for a long time. I stayed home, alone with my little ones, and all that work—just imagine! My father came with some folks to bring in the hay that lay on the ground. We had a threshing machine. I didn't have time to worry about Pyramus or what he was up to; all I noticed was that he wasn't barking as loudly at people. But after we'd finished with the second crop, and it came time to put the cows out to graze, I started to realize that he wasn't himself. I put the cows out at Le Raicart so I could keep an eye on them without leaving the house. I'd watch them from afar, and if one cow or another strayed, I'd just call out to Pyramus, since I left him there with them. That's how I came to realize that half the time he wasn't even in the pasture. That sly thing, he'd figured out that his master had left us and decided to take advantage of it. He used to care about only his home and his duties, always eager to do everything, but now he started to slack off, roaming far and wide. At first he'd be gone for just an hour or two, but soon it was all day long, and he'd come home only for his meals. I tried to punish him, but it never worked. Well, maybe I wasn't hitting him too hard, either. In any case, nothing could stop him from gallivanting about, neither kindness nor blows.

Here's how crafty he was. In 1915, when Hector came home on leave, Pyramus didn't leave the house the whole ten days he was here, except to accompany him when he went out. That dog never strayed from his side. And he was altogether the same dog as before, barking viciously at strangers and acting as if he were in charge of all our chores. But as soon as Hector's leave was over and he returned to the front, Pyramus went right back to his wandering ways; no four walls could hold him!

Toward the end of summer, some soldiers arrived who were stationed around here. Suddenly Pyramus knew no other masters: he'd hang around them constantly, even eat with them. Still, he'd check in with us briefly during the day, as if to catch up on the latest news. He'd be friendly to the children, but he didn't dare look my way, because he was ashamed, after all. Once in a while he'd sleep in his kennel at night, but not often. And then the soldiers left. One morning, I'd just gotten up, it was five o'clock and starting to drizzle. The soldiers were marching down the road, and I thought of my poor Hector. Behind the column of soldiers came the mule teams. All of a sudden, I spot my Pyramus, walking alongside a cart in the rain. I call him once, I call him twice. He stops, faces me, and I see him hang his head between his paws, as if he wants to come but can't and is ashamed. And I must say, he really looked upset. Then he made up his mind: he was going to catch up with the carts. I called him again; he stopped, but not for long, and pressed onward, with his head down and his tail, too, and his flanks drawn in. I watched him trot back to the column of soldiers, as they rounded the bend at the Chavignots' house. After that I never saw him again, ever.

The children missed Pyramus; they'd have liked to have another dog. I would have, too, but I had other things to think about: the work that never let up, the constant worry about my husband at the front—so many had fallen!—not to mention that I was about to give birth to my third child, your uncle Fernand, who came back two summers ago, after being a prisoner. These wars, there's no end to them.

It was in the summer of 1916 that my cousins from Villers-les-Bois came by one day and brought us a very young dog. It was two months old. We named it Belfort, but your mother, poor lamb—she was maybe, what, three? no more than that—she said "Béfort," and the name stuck. By the time Hector came home from the war in 1919, Béfort was a big handsome dog, strong as a horse, so to speak, and as tall as this table—I'm not exaggerating. He had a pretty blue coat sprinkled with white spots, and longish fur that curled at the neck and the ears. Such a handsome dog! Not only that, but good-natured and smart, too. He understood everything. Believe it or not, he'd often take care of the children for me—I could go out and work in the fields, and Béfort would watch them. He knew just as well as anyone what was off-limits for them: the pond, the manure pile, the slurry pit, the well, climbing up ladders. In fact, he's the one who taught your uncle Fernand to walk. You should have seen those two: the little one hanging on to his coat or his ear with one hand, without even looking, and the dog walking slowly, taking tiny steps and pausing whenever he felt the child hesitate.

Béfort was more than a dog: he was a person. When he saw that any of us was upset, he'd be even sadder than we were. He'd come lick our hands and look at us with eyes full of sorrow. If someone was crying, he'd cry, too, with a woeful little whine. I remember—how many times I saw it happen!—when Hector would make one of the children stand in the corner, Béfort would go, too, and stay there until the punishment was over. I tell you, animals like that, we really need more of them, to teach people how to love.

And as a herding dog, he had no equal. When it came time to put the cows to pasture in the commons, we led them out with him once, and after that he didn't need anyone's help, either to take them out or to watch over them. He kept them closely grouped as they walked along the road, and if a wagon came, he'd herd them aside in plenty of time, calmly and quietly, without hurrying. He wasn't like those ferocious dogs that are always jostling the animals, harassing them and barking them deaf. In the fields you'd never really see him run. He'd just give a bark now and then to let the cows know he was there. He'd raise his head and take a single step; that was all he had to do to restore order. The cows feared him—even respected him, I'd say.

Béfort had only a couple of faults, but they ended up causing him a lot of trouble: namely, his love of food and fighting. He was perhaps a bit of a prankster, too. There was hardly a day that he didn't fight with the local dogs, and he would always win. So you see how strong he was! People weren't too happy about it, but they didn't come and complain, either. After all, a dogfight isn't that serious. The only criticism they made from time to time, not too often and usually with a touch of humor, was that

Béfort was a thief—that he'd steal a bit of meat here, a bit of bacon there. We didn't quite believe it. He never stole at home; he wouldn't take the slightest thing unless we gave it to him. I began to wonder if they all weren't just jealous that we had such a fine dog.

On the other end of town, the Maufrelats had a big dog, about as big as Béfort, called César. I can't tell you exactly when they started meeting, but Béfort was probably about six. Since they were equally strong, their fights lasted a good long time. And then, after they'd finished fighting, little by little they became friends. At first they didn't do anything too terrible. They'd just run around together and pick fights with the other local dogs. But unfortunately, they didn't stop there. One day, Guste Bonardot's wife, Eléonore—the daughter of Léon Dominé and Esther Micoulin, whose first husband was Charles Masson, who was, in fact, my mother's cousin, since Eugène Masson, his father, was the half-brother of Jules Blot's wife, "lovely Amandine," we called her, a Bontemps; the Bontemps family came from Saint-Barain, and their youngest daughter, whose name I forget, married a Ragondet, from La Fragneuse, who was a relative—actually, a first cousin—so, a cousin of Xavier Millet, who was a wheelwright in the square where Justin Mignet now has his bicycle workshop . . . Now, what was I saying? Oh, that's right: Eléonore came over to complain that Béfort had stolen a string of sausages she had hanging in her kitchen, and, as a matter of fact, he'd done it with César, the Maufrelats' dog. Well, I defended Béfort in good faith, and I blamed the whole thing on César. The proof, I said to Eléonore, was that I have two andouilles hanging here, right by the fireplace, and Béfort never showed the least interest in them. All right, fine. Eight days go by, and then the butcher, Régis Belhomme, comes to call. Béfort and César had robbed him of a good five pounds of meat in one fell swoop. And after that, people were coming by every minute exclaiming about a calf's head, a ham, two pounds of blood sausage, what have you. Not a single pig was slaughtered without these two devils making off with their share, and always the choice morsels.

Who'd ever seen such shenanigans? One morning I was at the notary's with Hector, to deal with my uncle Amédée's estate, and I was sitting by the window chatting with my cousin Gabrielle. In the square, César, the Maufrelats' dog, was soaking up the sun, sprawled on a stone at the foot of the big cross; the butcher's bulldog was hanging around nearby. I still remember telling my cousin, "Look, there's César; Béfort's sure to arrive soon." All of a sudden, César rushes at the bulldog, and they're rolling on the ground. Hearing his dog barking, Belhomme looks up, grabs a club, and runs outside, pulling the shop gate closed behind him. The minute his back is turned, Béfort, who was hiding behind a woodpile, darts across the street, leaps over the gate, and comes back out with a leg of lamb in his mouth. Belhomme didn't see a thing. He was so proud at having chased away César, who now got to share the lamb.

After stunts like that, you can well imagine the trouble we were in. But what could we do? Beat Béfort? We just couldn't bring ourselves to, not even Hector. We all loved him too much. We tried tying him up, but he was so miserable and we felt bad—as if we didn't appreciate all he did for us. It weighed on our conscience. We tried it for one day; that was more than enough. So we let him free. But he and César kept up with their capers, and people kept coming over with their complaints, demands, and threats. Finally, it got to be too much. One day, in the spring of '24, the Mignards were about to marry off their eldest daughter. On the eve of the wedding, they were busy getting everything ready; their kitchen was filled with meat and poultry—you know how it is. We never knew quite how it happened, but we do know that Béfort and César made off with a quarter of mutton, as well as a goose the family had fattened especially for the occasion and had killed that very morning. Well, that was the last straw, obviously. We didn't know where to turn; the whole town was against us. We had to do something. There was a fellow named Ponard who'd come for the wedding and had a shop outside Paris. Seeing that we were in a fix, he offered to take Béfort away in his truck. So that's how we and Béfort were parted. You can imagine how it grieved us, but what else could we do? The day after he was gone, the Maufrelats found their César hanged from a tree along the road—a fate that Béfort had narrowly escaped.

A month went by—at least a month, because Xavier Millet was starting to make hay in his fields by the river. One evening, after supper, we were in the kitchen. Hector got up and said, "I'm going to bed." That's what he always said when he was about to go to bed. I was washing dishes at the sink, and your mother was drying them. I turned around and saw her white as a ghost, poor lamb, looking at the open window. "Béfort!" she cried. And, indeed, it was him. His two paws resting on the windowsill, he stuck his head inside and watched his people. He jumped right into the kitchen. Oh! it still makes me cry. How did he ever manage to make it back on his own? Just imagine: he was three hundred kilometers away, there was no one to show him the way, and of course he couldn't read the mileposts. How long the days must have seemed to him, so far from the people he loved!

We were all a bit worried, but so happy that we tried to reassure ourselves. Now that César was dead, he no longer had a partner to give him ideas, so perhaps he wouldn't go back to his old tricks. And, in fact, he kept out of trouble for almost a week. But it didn't last. He soon started up again, even worse than before. Just think, one day we found out he'd killed three chickens at the Poinsots'— folks who were already none too agreeable. The next day, it was two ducks at Céleste Reverchon's. During his long journey home he had to find food, you understand, so he got in the habit of taking fowl, which was the easiest, all along his way. And in the end he developed a taste for it, see. Well, you can imagine what a ruckus that caused around here. Now everyone feared for their hens, their geese, their ducks. People were all in a tizzy, and deep down, we could well understand it.

One afternoon I was washing clothes, and Béfort was lying beside me, near the laundry sink. Hector came into the courtyard with Grosbois, the gamekeeper, who had his rifle on his shoulder. Poor Hector, he was completely pale. He said, "Béfort, come here!" The dog looked at the rifle, then turned his sweet gaze to his master and me. He understood. Head down, he walked out beside Hector, right next to him. They left the courtyard with the gamekeeper and went down to the little meadow among the apple trees. I ran off to my kitchen. When I heard the two shots, I just cried and cried. Oh, how I cried!

For two years I didn't want another dog in the house. I was too upset about my Béfort. Then one day, your mother and I rode our bikes to Oussière to see Aunt Anna, who wasn't doing well, and that's when Uncle Adrien gave us Oscar. I didn't think much of the dog when I saw him, but your mother, poor lamb, I could see that she wanted him. She's the one who brought him home in a basket attached to her handlebars—you can imagine how small he was.

That dog, we never got anything out of him. He wasn't bad looking: white and yellow, with long legs. His face was handsome enough, but his eyes didn't speak to you. You couldn't find a lazier dog for miles around. A real cur, whose only interest was eating. We would have liked him to watch over the cows, but no way was he going to learn. Even pretending to watch them was too much for him. Nor would he guard the house—anyone could come in, night or day; it wasn't Oscar's affair. All he cared about was eating, gallivanting about to his heart's content, and sleeping in the sun, or in winter by the fire. What's more, he didn't like anyone, master or stranger; he was never affectionate, never even gave a friendly look. When you called him, he'd lift his head, see if there was any food to be had, and if not, he'd turn away. It was exactly as the saying goes: "Just like the dog that belongs to Paul / He runs the other way whenever you call."

Hector wanted to get rid of him, and for good reason;

that dog got on his nerves. But we kept him anyway, and the years went by, all too fast. And it was in '32 that misfortune struck. One evening, it was in autumn, Hector came home and went to bed. I'd noticed for a while that he didn't seem to have his usual vigor, but he wouldn't admit he was ill; he wanted to finish sowing the field. He went to bed without his supper, and eight days later he was gone. As my uncle Amédée used to say, being happy isn't a good sign; it just means that sadness missed the boat, but it'll be sure to come on the next one. Now, do you think Oscar felt any sorrow when his master died? It didn't mean a thing to him. Seeing that he had so little heart, I resented him.

Two years later, on a Sunday afternoon, toward evening, I was alone in the house. It was four o'clock in November and getting dark. Oscar was sleeping there, under the furnace. Who should pull up in the courtyard but Dominique, the smuggler, in his dogcart, with Jules la Marmite. Jules was a rather pathetic sort: a drunkard, a loafer who'd work only when he needed to; the rest of the time you'd find him fishing, hanging around cafés, or gambling. I heard he once lost fifty-two francs in an afternoon playing with Félicien Roux. I'm talking about ten years ago. The other fellow, Dominique, wasn't from around here, and where he was from no one ever knew. He was a rogue, and a big man, too; he barely fit under the door, with his red beard and his eyes that were always full of anger. You can imagine how uneasy I was, at home all alone with those ruffians here. They were already a bit drunk, bellowing in my kitchen and trying to sell me their smuggled goods. Oscar, of course, didn't budge; whatever might happen to me, he couldn't care less. I resented him. As it turns out, Dominique had come to talk to me about him: that breed, he says, is only good for harnessing, and he offered to trade him for a nine-month-old shepherd that was snarling at the yoke.

Oscar didn't quite understand what was happening. I was even a bit sad to let him go off with strangers. It was almost dark. I couldn't really see him leaving. The dog team was barking, Dominique cracked his whip, swearing, and the cart took off down the road. After leaving here, my two ne'er-do-wells went around begging for money. Then they went drinking at La Frisée's till all hours, and what a state they were in when they left! As they were nearing Guillemin's place, around two or three in the morning, Jules was so drunk that Dominique laid him down on the cart. Oscar wasn't the most energetic dog in the team as it was, and now he simply refused to go on. In a rage, Dominique unharnessed him and started kicking him and beating him with the handle of his whip. A drunken man loses all reason, and even at his calmest, Dominique was cruel. The more the dog howled, the angrier he got. Finally, he went at Oscar with his knife. They buried him at the side of the road. It was no great loss, of course, but I hadn't traded him away to have him so abused.

The dog that Dominique had left with me that day was a pretty black shepherd with sweet, timid eyes, the look of an animal that's been beaten. What his name was you already know, I don't need to tell you. As soon as he came into our home, he was happy to be here, and he gave us his love. No idler, this one; he quickly took to proper duties as a dog. To be sure, he didn't have Béfort's intelligence, or even Pyramus's; the cows were hardly afraid of him. Nor were the other animals: the cats always got along well with him, and I remember one little white hen that used to sleep between his paws. He was never mean at all. But I'm not going to start talking about Finaud, because you know him. Of course, he's not what he used to be. Now that he's going on fourteen, and his hair's all gray and he can barely drag himself along, he's just an old guy. But even so, he's kept his character, which was never like any other. Because, you see, there's something many people don't know: that there's almost more difference between dogs than between people. I mean in terms of their inner nature, what comes from the heart and from the head.

All right, your socks are dry now. It's time to think about doing your homework. But before you do, go to the woodshed and fetch me some wood, and break some twigs to light the fire tomorrow morning.

Translated by Rose Vekony

A Lively Little Tune
Didier Daeninckx

EVERY DAY, whatever the weather, Eusèbe Sormulin takes his bicycle down from the hook, limps along the stable with its leaky roof, and stops next to the stump he splits his wood on. Clinging to a low beam, he climbs onto the bike, then uses his other hand to lift his stiff leg over the crossbar. He had the Urcel blacksmith remove the right pedal and weld in its place a jerry-rigged footrest that exactly fits the heel of his boot. Eusèbe settles himself in the saddle, then shoves off hard from the beam to gain the momentum he needs to get underway. He's lucky: the family farm, which his father still runs, sits right at the top of the Filain hill, a steep path that even tough guys have to climb on foot. The morning sky is a clear blue, as it was the day before. Eusèbe Sormulin cranks the pedal

DIDIER DAENINCKX (1949–) is a prizewinning writer of novels, young adult books, graphic novels, and short stories. He has a fondness for detective stories rooted in history and political reality, and his take on daily life is tragic and ironic, but often enlivened by gallows humor. Daeninckx also works as an investigative reporter for an online daily, amnistia.net. This short story is from *Histoire et faux-semblants* (2007).

with his powerful good leg, using the hundred-odd yards of level ground to get going fast enough to make it up the slope to the plateau.

For about ten minutes, he's alone on the ridge, where the wind is vainly trying to raise a little dust. It's only at that moment, when he's free of the anxiety about setting out, that he becomes a *maréchal* in an army of shadows. Coasting along on his bike, he can hear the murmurs in the Laon countryside, the clatter of weapons, the whinnying of harnessed mounts, the fits of coughing from those who smoked too much or caught cold. This is a moment that recurs every day of his watch. He commands invisible troops dug in along the Aisne and Ailette rivers, but no order ever passes his lips. His silence spares them every day.

Edmond Goulphe has no idea what thoughts are going around under his partner's kepi. He comes up from Vailly on the other slope along a less demanding route, and he has the use of both his legs. From dawn to dusk, winter and summer, the two men crisscross the Chemin des Dames battlefield from the Soissons road junction as far as Corbeny on the main road between Reims and Laon. In the last few years, the farmers have gradually been taking back land once plowed by dueling artillery fire. It's said they secretly sacrifice part of their first harvest of wheat, barley, corn, and alfalfa because they're convinced that the plants' roots have sunk into the flesh and blood of soldiers mowed down by the shooting. Plows keep hitting buried shells and turning up skeletal remains, rusty helmets, scraps of field jackets, shattered rifle stocks. In the beginning, Prussian soldiers were brought in by young

French draftees, who watched from a distance as the others cleared the bombs. The Germans would pile the high explosives in a crater, remove their detonators, and blow them up all at once. That's when Eusèbe Sormulin and Edmond Goulphe had to be especially vigilant. They would flush out skinny kids from Bray, Cerny, or Oulches from where they had hidden in the folds of the land to watch the fireworks. Ten years earlier, a dozen spectators and as many bomb squad members had been cut to pieces when a pile of munitions exploded prematurely. A piece of shrapnel slammed into Eusèbe's knee, but whenever he feels tempted by self-pity because of his stiff leg, he has only to think of that kid from Vendresse blinded by the metal shards. Eusèbe sees him each time he goes down to fish in the Viel-Arcy swamps.

Whenever they request it, a truck comes up onto the plateau to take the chemical weapons away to the north, where they're buried in abandoned mine shafts between Lens and Arras. Mustard gas wreaked devastation on the hills of the battlefield, and every time someone digs up a gas canister, Edmond trots out the ritual joke, as if to conjure fate: "They should plant grapes there, it's got the right exposure. Besides, no need to sweat trying to make it into proper Champagne, the grapes'll be naturally carbonated!"

At noon, the partners stop at the Cerny crossroads, alone in the middle of this deserted high ground that nobody wants anymore, even though men once spent years dying for it by the thousands. They hunker down out of the wind in the ruins of the sugar refinery, light a fire of twigs, and heat their lunch buckets. They eat without exchanging a word, like resigned infantrymen before an assault. They light a cigarette with a hot coal and share it, then Edmond helps his partner onto his bike, handlebars pointed toward Craonne. This is their main job: to provide security, chase curious people away, stop kids from playing at war with scraps of matériel still found in the pillboxes thirteen years after the end of the fighting. They understand all those people; they're protecting them against themselves. What they don't get, on the other hand, are the battlefield rats, the cemetery scavengers, the body collectors—the scum who prey on the remains, or worse, who enjoy displaying fragments of the lives of the dead. They caught one a few months ago, a pharmacist's assistant from Soissons, who came to the hillsides only after nightfall. He was equipped with French Sixth Army topo maps that he'd bought secondhand on a Lille sidewalk and was checking out the most secret positions, looking for skeletons so he could pull their gold teeth. He wasn't even doing it for money. After Eusèbe and Edmond arrested him, their colleagues in Soissons searched the man's house and found several hundred gold molars, incisors, and canines, carefully listed and classified according to criteria as obscure as the urge to collect such trophies.

As they approached Craonnelle, Edmond pedaled hard to get a few dozen meters ahead. He hopped off his bike near the steep path leading to the abbey, stood with his legs spread before a wind-beaten bush, closed his eyes, and watered the parched earth. He opened his eyelids and was buttoning his fly as the squeaking of Eusèbe's bicycle grew louder. That was when he saw the man kneeling between two rows of saplings at the edge of the Vauclair forest,

in that no-man's-land where vegetation hadn't yet managed to extend its domain. He turned and raised his arm,
then slowly waved up and down, signaling his partner to
stop. Eusèbe rode straight for a road sign and grabbed it
as he passed, using it to brace himself as he stepped down.
Hunched over, he limped to his partner, who pointed to
the motionless gray figure below them.

"What's he fiddling with, d'you think?"

"I don't know, he's half hidden by the leaves. Hand me
your binoculars."

Edmond adjusted them to his eyes and turned the
thumbscrew with the tip of his middle finger. The man,
crouched in the distance below, had moved a little to the
right.

"Can you see what he's up to?"

"Yeah, he's digging with a stone. He dug up a helmet
and a piece of cloth. There are also pieces of wood on the
side, but they could just as easily be bones. For the rest,
you better look for yourself, otherwise you won't believe
me."

Eusèbe took the binoculars in turn, focusing as he
pointed them at his target.

"I can't believe it! What the hell's he up to? This is the
first time we've come across a black guy. What do we do?"

"I'll try heading for the poachers' path, the one that
runs along the swamp. I'll get behind him and flush him
out, so he won't have any choice but to climb up to you.
You better stay here with your gun out to grab him. I don't
think he's armed, but it's best to be careful with these
creeps. First wrong move he makes, shoot to kill. In the
report, I'll say you gave him the usual warnings."

Edmond moved away, bent over and screened by the

dry grass. He reached shelter behind an old stack of logs shredded by flying bullets, then circled around the man, who was still busy with his digging. He unintentionally flushed some quail hidden deep in the old furrows, and had to hit the dirt, his heart pounding, when they took off. His chin scraped by the hard earth, Edmond peered through the weeds and saw that the man merely glanced at the beating wings against the cloudless sky. He crawled forward and stood up when he felt he was within range. Then he blew with all his might into his whistle's tiny mouthpiece, the shrill sound making his own eardrums vibrate. He spat it out then held his pistol at arm's length, pointed at the scavenger.

"Hey, you! Drop the stone! Hands in the air, and stand up slowly. Don't try anything smart. You do something funny and I won't hesitate to shoot."

Still pointing his gun, Edmond crossed some of the distance separating him from the African. The man displayed his pale, dusty palms, and slowly got to his feet. The corolla made by his long coat narrowed as he stood up. Through the gap, you could see that he was almost naked under the wool coat. Eusèbe hobbled toward them, raising a little yellow cloud each time he propelled his right leg forward. The man didn't resist when they arrested and handcuffed him, just stared at them with dark, deep-set eyes. Broken bones were sticking out of his pocket. Edmond's father had spent five years knocking around the French colonies in North Africa. Once back in Champagne, he'd commanded a squad of the 9th Zouave Regiment and had been part of the 16 April 1917 offensive near the Paradis wood, whose branches they could see. He and his men took Chivy in a river of blood, while the 418th Infantry Regiment, which was within hailing distance and trying to hold the Misaine trench near the sugar refinery, was being cut up by the German bombardment. Edmond had heard his father tell how his squad mate Sergeant Paoli had died, and heard him praise the bravery of his North African *sidis* and his *fellagha*. He'd communicated with them with a rudimentary vocabulary, a way of talking Edmond now adopted.

"You speak French?"

The man chose to answer in the same mode.

"Yes, me speak French. Me baptized."

Then Eusèbe took over

"You from where? Senegal? Upper Volta?"

The prisoner nodded, playing for time.

"Senegal."

"Why you steal bones of dead?"

"You're wrong, I wasn't stealing the bones of the dead. I can explain. Listen to me."

Blind with rage, Edmond didn't notice the change of register. He lunged at the black man and yanked a broken tibia bone from his open coat pocket.

"So what the hell is this, a toothpick? Come on, let's get going. And no funny business."

Edmond gave Eusèbe a leg up onto his bicycle. On either side of the African, they walked down to the Craonne mayor's office, which was flanked by a firehouse and a guardhouse to hold prisoners before their transfer to Soissons. The African stood near the door, chest and legs bare, a scrap of colored cloth around his hips. His long coat lay on a small table. They carefully inventoried the contents of his pockets: the tibia fragment, a few knucklebones, a piece of a skull, and a kind of string with animal teeth, fish bones, coral, and tiny metal rings threaded on it. No papers, no money. He refused to answer the questions put to him, just confirming the country he was from, Senegal. Eusèbe opened the cell door and shoved him into the gloom, then tossed his coat in after him.

"We'll come back and see you this evening. Maybe you'll be more talkative."

The cell was already occupied by a copper scavenger, a repeat offender who'd been caught filling a cart with shells dug out of the banks of the Ailette near Crandelain, where he lived.

"Hello, pal. There's just one bench, and I'm using it. What the hell were you doing, digging up skeletons? Human remains aren't worth a damn thing."

The African remained silent. He put on his overcoat and went to sit in a corner of the cell.

"Suit yourself. My name's Gaston Pilcourt. I used to work for guys from where you're from. It was in Paris, boulevard Kellermann, at the 23rd Colonial Infantry Regiment depot. My job was to fix whatever broke down. Ever hear of Bakary Diallo? He's Senegalese, like you."

"No."

Pilcourt pulled out a pack of Gauloises, offered one to his cellmate, who took it, and lit them with a match he scratched on the wall.

"I came back home to take over the farm on the Chemin des Dames three years ago, after my father died. But farming's so hard, you can starve standing up. Ain't nothin' harder. I soon figured out I could make more money collecting precious metal than waiting for the wheat to ripen. Want me to be honest with you? I think you were bullshitting those two cops. You don't look Senegalese. You look more like the guys from Madagascar who used to live in the rue de Rennes depot. Am I right?"

The African blew out a long puff of smoke, which caught the sunlight slanting down from the high window.

"Yeah, you're right. I've never been to Africa. I come from little village called Tendo, deep in the northern mountains right above Tiendanite, upstream along the river."

Gaston Pilcourt ground the cigarette on the sole of his shoe.

"Never heard of it. Where is that, in the Caribbean?"

His cellmate pointed to the ground.

"It's right there, but on the other side, in New Caledonia. My name's Wanakaeni. It's from Lifou, my grandmother's place, but the Mixed Pacific Regiment officers just used the first part, Wana."

"I can't believe it!" the farmer broke in. "Were you in Hurtebise, that hellhole right next to here, in April '17?"

"Not far from it. We were to the west of the Poteau d'Ailles. In three days we lost more than five hundred of our guys around the farm. For nothing. I came here to look for the remains of my brother, my cousins, and the members of my tribe, to honor them. We'd been forced to leave them behind, gutted like dead fish. Not a single one wanted to come here; they had to stick a bayonet to our backs to force us onto the boat."

The door suddenly swung open. Eusèbe came up to the bars, followed by Edmond carrying a jug, a loaf of bread, and two slices of corned beef wrapped in brown paper.

"Go easy on your rations. A car's coming to get you early tomorrow afternoon."

As soon as they were gone, Pilcourt pulled out his pack of Gauloises again and shook two cigarettes out through the torn opening.

"I don't get why they had to threaten you. You're French, aren't you?"

"Not quite, just a 'French subject.' But I'm a Kanak all the same. I was born one year before the turn of the century, and was shipped out aboard the *Gange*, feeling none too happy about it. For months I'd seen our older brothers coming back—not all of them, of course, only those who'd been discharged. We'd never have imagined that France would give them back to us in that state. Up to then, nobody had ever seen someone without an arm or legs, or with half their face missing. It just didn't exist! Isamatro's son didn't have any jaw left, just a hole where he stuck pieces of yam and taro. It made people feel so bad, they made excuses not to eat with him anymore. His father made him a kind of little flap to hide the wound. He would stick his hands underneath it. We couldn't get used to it. He was in agony, we could hear him screaming in his hut at night, but no doctor ever came to see him. For months, every able-bodied man under forty-five was being drafted. If you didn't want to be taken, you had to be sick as a dog or run off into the jungle, with the Tahitians on your heels. They caught me on the Hienghène trail, beat me, then took me in chains to a tramp steamer we called "The Coaster" because it circled around the island loading "volunteers." Before being shipped out on the *Gange*, I spent three months in the boulevard Extérieur prison, under the courthouse. This is heaven by comparison!"

Pilcourt broke the loaf in half, ripped off two pieces

the size of a large apple, and handed one to Wanakaeni. He set the package with the corned beef on the corner of the bench.

"Help yourself. I don't know about you, pal, but I'm starting to feel a little empty space in my belly and I don't want it to get any bigger. For water, we'll just have to drink from the jug. All's fair in love and war."

He tore off a piece of gelatinous meat, set it on the bread, and chewed in silence for a moment. Then he leaned toward the Kanak.

"They could've shot you, put a bullet in your back for desertion."

"When I was at Craonne, Cerny, and Poteau d'Ailles, I must've wished they'd done that a thousand times, believe me. It wasn't worth living through anything I saw there. The problem is that we Kanaks were considered 'volunteers.' The truth is, the chiefs of our tribes just pointed us out to the recruiters in exchange for a couple of bills and a pile of tobacco. They wound up regretting it."

"Why? Were there reprisals?"

Wanakaeni laughed as he tore a piece of paper and took his share of the meat.

"No need. For years they were left to face the women and the old people, and I wouldn't wish that on my worst enemy. Actually, what happened is that the countryside emptied out. The fields went to seed, diseases like plague and leprosy attacked people's weakened bodies. And fear skulked around the villages."

Pilcourt tipped his head back, opened his mouth, and took a long slug of cool water.

"Because of wild animals?"

"In New Caledonia, men are the only wild animals. All along the coast, from Boat-Pass Point to Pouembout, it's nothing but one jail after another, crammed with robbers and killers that France got rid of by shipping them to the ends of the earth. When their sentences were up, most of them weren't able to get a boat back. So they settled there, a little ways away from the villages. Needless to say, they weren't the most desirable of neighbors. When I got back home in July 1919, I didn't recognize my side of the mountain."

The copper scavenger stuck his hand in his pants pocket and pulled out a dozen butts. He ripped them open, shook out the tiny flakes of tobacco, and divided and sorted it onto two strips of newspaper. He rolled two cigarettes, with printing on their sides.

"Did the convicts move onto your land while you were away?"

"No, they kept their heads down. In the fall of 1917 the entire north rebelled against the recruitment. Even the lepers and the blind took up weapons. The French soldiers attacked Oubatche, then Tiendanite, helped by the Tahitians. They burned everything in their path—the huts and the crops. My wife's mother, a Tjibaou, tried to escape with a group by going up the river between the cliffs, toward Tendo. The weather was colder than anybody on the island could remember. The soldiers tracked them, waited for morning, then shot them like rabbits when they went down to a pool to get water. They found her in the stream with her skull shattered and her youngest son, a kid five years old, a stone's throw from his mother's body, howling."

It was quite dark by the time Wanakaeni told Pilcourt about the death of Noël, the head of the Kanak rebels.

"They were on his trail, he hadn't eaten anything in nearly two days and was wandering close to his tribe, in an area called the Tiamou. He knocked on the door of the man he knew well and trusted, Mohammed Ben Ahmed. He'd been an ordinary criminal, not one of those Algerian deportees who rose up against the French when they were enlisting Arabs to fight the Prussians in 1870. Ben Ahmed shot him five times with his pistol, but Noël still managed to get out of the house and walk toward the river. The traitor finished him off at the foot of a mango tree in a place called Goropûrûmô. He took a sickle and cut his head off, just like they did to Ataï, the Kanak leader who died in the big 1878 uprising."

The next morning, gunshots awoke Wanakaeni, who threw off his coat and jumped to his feet. His cellmate was already awake, enjoying an early smoke while eating some bread soaked in what remained of the water.

"Relax. It's nearly Bastille Day, and the kids around here can't wait to set off their firecrackers. You hungry?"

"Thanks, I'm fine. I wanted to ask you: were you in the war?"

Pilcourt started to walk from one wall to the next, feet splayed.

"Yes, but at the rear, thanks to my mother. I was born with flat feet. Here, look: in a parade, you'd think they'd enlisted a duck! That's how I wound up at the Twenty-third Colonial Infantry Regiment depot, on boulevard Kellermann. What about you? Were Cerny and Poteau d'Ailles as bad as they say?"

"No, they were worse. The only ones who could say for sure aren't here to talk about it, like Wahéa, an infantryman: we found his heart stuck in the top branches of a tree after a German bombardment. We were fighting under Colonel Maroix, who replaced Lieutenant Colonel Lofler, who died on the Somme in 1916. On the morning of April 16 they took us to the Troyon Ravine, halfway up the hill. The goal was to take the six lines of enemy trenches. At six in the morning we had to get up and begin the assault. There was a hillock ringed by barbed wire two hundred yards below the crest of the hill. We took the first trench, which was called Bonn, and that's when things started looking bad. We were under fire from two machine guns, one up on the plateau and the other hidden behind a spur. We couldn't see them. And they had more matériel at the Caverne du Dragon and the Trou d'Enfer. They were cutting us to pieces. We reached the second trench, the one they called Ems, but leaving a slew of dead behind us. Nearly six hundred in three days of fighting. We never even saw the third trench. And we had to hang on until we were relieved, and the whole time we were being shot to pieces. A few days later we learned that some forty French soldiers had hidden in a hollow when their officer signaled the attack, and that a dozen others had abandoned their positions at the front line. I think some were condemned to death. I don't blame them, they weren't cowards. Me, I tried to slip away in New Caledonia, and the only reason I didn't do it here in Champagne is that I didn't know where to go. All this, just to find myself in jail in Craonne fourteen years later! I recognized the landscape when the cops marched me down here. It looks the same, even though the trees have grown back."

Gaston Pilcourt began to whistle a nostalgic tune, then started singing. The lyrics were:

> *The ones who come back will be the ones with the*
> *dough*
> *'Cause they're the ones we're croaking for.*
> *But that's all over, because the troops*
> *Are all going out on strike.*
> *It'll be your turn, you fat bastards,*
> *To climb up to the plateau,*
> *'Cause if you want to go to war*
> *Put your own damn skins on the line.*

Wanakaeni's eyes widened. "Where'd you learn that song?"

"Can't remember. From a friend, I guess. It's *La chanson de Craonne*. You sing it in New Caledonia, too?"

The Kanak shook his head.

"This is the first time I've heard the tune, but I know the lyrics. When the survivors came down from Hurtebise, Cerny, and Ailles, we rested for a while behind the lines not far from Craonne. There were some Moroccan infantrymen there, some Zouaves, and a few guys from the 418th Infantry Regiment. I found myself next to a soldier who was writing in his notebook. He read me what you just sang. When I asked him if he was going to set it to music, he said that he couldn't do it but that his brother in Paris was sure to find a lively little tune to go with his text."

Pilcourt put his arm on Wanakaeni's shoulder.

"'A lively little tune,' is that what he said? A lively little tune . . ."

The Kanak was about to confirm this when the door opened, flooding the cell with light. Edmond Goulphe turned the key in the lock and pulled the bars aside. Eusèbe Sormulin stepped in, looking Pilcourt up and down.

"You'll be here a little longer. Your transfer to Soissons is for this afternoon."

Then he limped over to the "African."

"As for you, Wanakaeni, you're leaving now. We know the whole story. A car's taking you back where you came from."

As Wanakaeni stepped out of the Craonne municipal guardroom, some kids' firecrackers startled him. Three men were waiting next to a black Hotchkiss. The driver picked up the main road, crossed Reims, and headed for Paris. Three hours later, the sedan stopped in front of the Jardin d'Acclimatation zoo, which was thronged with visitors to the Colonial Exhibition. Wanakaeni had escaped from it a week earlier, and he now rejoined the hundred other Kanaks living in a pen between the crocodile pool and the wild animal cages, forced to pretend they were man-eaters.

A few weeks later, when the crocodiles accidentally died, the veteran of the Mixed Pacific Regiment and two dozen of his fellows were swapped for some alligators from the Hagenbeck Circus in Cologne. So for a few months, before a ship took the Kanaks back to Nouméa, Germans who had lost their colonies along with the war got their thrills throwing peanuts to the French cannibals.

Translated by William Rodarmor

The Lottery of France

Dominique Jamet

NOT ALL CASTLES ARE IN THE AIR.

I once knew a man who, for twenty-five years, indulged in the perfectly legal but nonetheless immoral practice of buying lottery tickets. Nothing in his otherwise honorable, open, and well-ordered existence would lead you to suspect this hidden vice. He didn't bet on horses or soccer games; he didn't play cards or go bowling; he wasn't a member of any club; he'd never even once stepped into a casino. At most, he might scrape the silver foil off a scratch-and-win card when he felt the urge, with no more expectation than the payoff it offered, which wasn't much.

But no matter where or how busy he was, and whatever

DOMINIQUE JAMET (1936–) is a writer and journalist who has worked as a reporter or editor at *France Soir*, *Combat*, *l'Aurore*, *Le Figaro Littéraire*, and *Le Quotidien de Paris*, among others, and played an important role in the creation of France's national library. His novels include *Antoine et Maximilien* (1986), *Le nouveau Candide* (1994), and *Un château sur le sable* (1998). This story is Jamet's contribution to a 2002 anthology, *Contes de campagne*.

the weather, he never missed the time-consuming chore of filling in and submitting lottery tickets. When necessary, he didn't hesitate to make the fifty-kilometer trip to the nearest lottery office. On holidays he might travel clear across Paris to find an outlet that was still open, trembling at the thought of getting there only to find the window shut. And he would watch for the results of the two weekly drawings or have someone inform him as soon as possible. They were held on Wednesdays and Saturdays. The first drawing was for small change; there were many winning tickets, but it was small change nonetheless. The second drawing was serious business, however. Winning it could change the lucky person's life forever.

Filling out the tickets involved entering three series of seven numbers twice a week, for a total of twelve combinations a week, which were valid for both drawings. Added to this, in the interests of being comprehensive, were the special tickets issued on Friday the thirteenth, on the days of the World Cup final of the soccer championship in the honors division, after return matches, and on every other national holiday.

Our man naturally felt that the lottery was too serious to be left to chance. So he filled out the tickets on a biweekly basis in accordance with certain immutable laws.

The first of the series contained three numbers; here he entered the year, month, and day of his birth and two times two numbers corresponding to the month and the day of his wife and daughter's birthdays. Always playing these same numbers gave him an unbreakable bond to the lottery. He couldn't bear the idea that "his" numbers might be chosen on a day when he had neglected to fill out a lottery ticket. The second series of numbers was given over to spontaneity, improvisation, disorder. More often than not, he left that one in the hands of the ticket seller—using the system popularly known as "flash lottery." The third series was the fruit of long and erudite calculations, which, sadly, never paid off.

In the face of these repeated disappointments, our man's nearest and dearest—the only people he told about his secret life—would often tease him about his innocent obsession, his hopes so unceasingly dashed, his illusions so regularly revived, and the small fortunes he so regularly wasted in the consuming fires of the lottery. At first he would let them talk. He was rational enough to admit that his chances of winning—really winning—were, if not equal to zero, then infinitely close to it. But, when his back was to the wall, he would pull the irrefutable weapon of logic out of his arsenal. The only people who were totally, definitively, and irrevocably sure not to win the lottery, he argued, were those who didn't play it.

At heart, he despaired of sharing his true motivation and hopes with such pedestrian personalities, or of helping them understand it so that they, too, could be initiated into his system.

So, what exactly did he expect from the French national lottery? Certainly not material gain. That venerable public institution wasn't in the business of philanthropy, he knew. Its primary mission wasn't to put money into the hands of millions of gamblers, but to swell the state's coffers and, incidentally, to provide for the comfort of the lottery administrators. Our man only asked that, for a

modest sum, it stimulate his desires, feed his imagination, and provide him twice a week with dreams that carried him from Wednesday night through Saturday night,
when he lost his money, and then again from Saturday
night to Wednesday night, when he lost again. A small
price to pay for an obsession.

His real obsession, you see, took the shape of a house.
A beautiful house in France. A house somewhere in the
beautiful French countryside. All the beautiful houses
in France, in fact, which he couldn't otherwise afford.
With his lottery ticket in his pocket, he visited them in
his mind, bought them with confidence, inhabited them
in his fantasies, and furnished them in his head. He created a life for himself, a thousand peaceful, charmed lives,
bathed in sunshine, enlivened by children's laughter, with
a stunning view of forest, sea, mountains, and happiness.

Thus, galloping about on his wonderful steed wherever
he pleased, along winding paths and beside lazy rivers,
sometimes armed only with a photo from a magazine
or a laudatory description glimpsed in the window of a
real estate agency, he gradually amassed a considerable
amount of property—a fantastic amount of property, I
might even say.

His first acquisition, a longtime favorite, was a low,
whitewashed house with dark blue shutters. Above the
door, which was painted the same dark blue, a lamp with
a plain enamel reflector gazed at the reflection of the
house itself in the black waters of one of the canals of
the Marais in Poitou, just like a painting by Magritte.
He hated the influx of Parisian snobs to the Ile de Ré,
but couldn't resist the family house discreetly tucked

away near the café terrace opposite the church in Ans.
To that, he added the seventeenth-century mansion in a
leafy bower on the rue de Sully in Saint-Martin. From
the terrace of his home in Gordes, he could watch the
sunset gild the shimmering hills of the Luberon; from
the garden of his farmhouse in Aix, he could see the rising sun turn Mount Sainte-Victoire pink. He let himself
be seduced by the austere facade of one house because its
back door opened onto a hidden garden in the heart of
Mortagne. The warm brown roofs of Semur-en-Auxois
charmed him; he fell in love with the old police station in
Domme. He opened a low door half hidden by ivy, almost
invisible in a gray stone wall, went down six timeworn
steps, and found the water of the Loire, vast and familiar,
lapping against the levee. He pushed a wicket open, took
three steps across the sand, and walked into the warm,
pellucid waters of Palombaggia. Pine needles crunched
under his feet, crickets filled the undergrowth with their
deafening din, and with thundering, earthshaking blows
the ocean beat against eternity at the end of the path. He
couldn't decide which he liked best, his villa in Hossegor
or his cabin in Cap-Ferret.

He had a long low farmstead in Perche; a half-timber
house perched high in Hochwald, a lavish charterhouse in
Saint-Emilion, and a beautiful, melancholy villa in Char-
treuse. He completely refurbished a superb ruin in Saint-
Arcons and a pirate's stronghold in the Ile-aux-Moines.
In short, he had all the advantages, all the delights, all
the pleasure of owning property without any of its incon-
veniences. He was not troubled by litigious neighbors,

unwanted visitors, frozen pipes, leaky roofs, burglars, or property and capital gains taxes.

The man who loved houses never won the lottery. The man who played the lottery was a lifelong renter who never owned a house. But throughout his life he desired, coveted, and possessed France in all her beauty, richness, and diversity, under the very noses of her actual owners. Nothing belonged to him, everywhere was home.

In smiling on him, fortune had spared him the cruelest of constraints, of having to make a choice.

Translated by Anna Livia

EDITORS

WILLIAM RODARMOR (1942–) is a journalist, editor, and French literary translator. One of his many book translations, *Tamata and the Alliance,* by solo sailor Bernard Moitessier, won the 1996 Lewis Galantière Award from the American Translators Association. His most recent translations are *Julien Parme,* by Florian Zeller (2008), *Diasporas,* by Stéphane Dufoix (2008), and *The Book of Time,* by Guillaume Prévost (2007). He lives in Berkeley, California, and took over the editing of this book after Anna Livia's untimely death.

ANNA LIVIA (1955–2007) taught French and linguistics at the University of California, Berkeley. She was a scholar, novelist, and translator, and also a dedicated feminist. Among her translations are *Lucie Delarue Mardrus, The Angel and the Perverts,* and *A Perilous Advantagean,* an anthology of writings by Natalie Clifford Barney. Her novel, *Bruised Fruit* (1999) was shortlisted for a Lammy award. Two earlier books—*Minimax* (1991) and *Incidents Involving Mirth* (1990)—were short-listed for the same award.

TRANSLATORS

Jean Anderson, Neil Blackadder, Linda Coverdale, C. Dickson, and Rose Vekony contributed translations to this volume. For biographical information about these translators, please visit our website (www.whereaboutspress.com).